W9-BXA-711

love is a
many
trousered
thing

Confessions of
GEORGIA NICOLSON

LOUISE RENNISON

love is a many trousered thing

confessions of GEORGIA NICOLSON

HARPER TEEN
An Imprint of HarperCollins Publishers

Library of Congress Cataloging-in-Publication Data is available.
ISBN 978-0-06-085387-7 (trade bdg.) — ISBN 978-0-06-085388-4 (lib. bdg.)

Typography by Alison Donalty
1 2 3 4 5 6 7 8 9 10
❖
First Edition
Visit Georgia at www.georgianicolson.com

With deep luuurve to all the usuals. I'm not saying
I'm bored with you, or that you are all usual because,
believe me, you're not. Anyway, can we get on . . .

P.S. Thank you and blimey to Mr. Urrrrr.

A Note from Georgia

Dearest international and marvy chummly wummlies,

Yes, once again I have given you my all (oo-er), so here is *Love Is a Many Trousered Thing*. And it is, believe me.

I wanted it to be called *Trouser Snakes-a-gogo!* but the grown-ups said that was too rude. I had the same trouble with *And That's When It Fell Off in My Hand*—the Hamburger-a-gogo "grown-ups" said *that* was too rude.

I said, "How do you mean? Do you mean that you think it might be something about a boy's trouser-snake addenda?"

And they said, "Yes."

And I said, "But if that came off in your hand, that would not be a comedy diary, that would be a medical book." But you can't tell people.

So you see how vair, vair tiring the whole thing can be. But I struggle out of my bed of pain again only because I luuurve you all so much.

Lots of kisses, but not in a lezzie way,

Georgia xxx

P.S.
You will also notice that Jas has introduced the idea of virtual upper-body fondling to the snogging scale. This is typical of what I have to put up with.
P.P.S.
If you have a Jas in your life, EAT HER—it's the only sensible thing to do.
P.P.P.S.
Even though I'm vair, vair tired, it's come to my attention that there are some people who haven't read my diaries before and keep asking me stuff about the ace gang, and the snogging scale, and disco inferno dancing. So for those vair, vair lazy people, I've added some lists of things at the back of the book.

love is a
many
trousered
thing

hoooorn!!!

saturday july 16th

11:45 p.m.

Run away, run away!!!

Pant, pant, pant.

And double pants.

How in the name of God's novelty under-crackers and matching toga have I ended up running along the streets at midnight?

I'll tell you how. You wait ages for a Sex God to come along and then two come along at the same time. Where is the sense in that? If it is all part of Big G's divine plan, all I can say is this: "Keep it simple, Big G. Just give me one Sex God to eat at a time. And then if I am not full up, I'll have another one. Thank you. Regards to Baby Jesus."

That is all I am saying. Inwardly, obviously, as I am nearly dead with trying to run in my high-heel boots. I may have to lie down in a ditch in a minute.

11:50 p.m.

I had to stop and sit in the hedge by the park. I'm so out of breath. Hurrah, I am sitting in the dark like a panting vole in a skirt.

three minutes later

Pant, pant. So this is a brief résumé of vole girl's evening.

Scene 1

A top night at the Stiff Dylans gig, including an excellent Viking disco inferno dance* in honor of Rosie and Sven's forthcoming (well, in eighteen years' time) wedding, Sven arriving in furry shorts and, as the *pièce de* whatsit, Masimo, lead singer and Luuurve God that I have been dreaming of and longing for, asked me to go outside, and said, "So, Signorína Georgia, I am free man for you. If you still want for us to go out."

Keep in mind that he said it in his gorgey porgey Pizza-a-gogo land accent. Looking at me like I was a Sex Kitty.

---

*Note to the dim (and I mean this in a loving way)—the Viking disco inferno dance goes stamp, stamp to the left, left leg kick, kick, arm up, stab, stab to the left, and HOOOOOOORN!

Scene 2

Just as I was experiencing Swoon City and melty pantaloonies a car pulled up and Robbie the original Sex God got out.

The one who had left me and gone to Kiwi-a-gogo land.

To snog marsupials and so on for the rest of his life.

Not.

Scene 3

After a moment of silence I said in a quick-thinking and casual way, "Oh hello, Robbie, do excuse me, I have a train to catch and time and tide wait for no man."

And walked quickly off before breaking into a slight trot. Then a light gallop. Then I ended up in the hedge and that is where all this started.

In conclusion I would say that after queuing up at the cakeshop of luuurve for ages I have accidentally bought two cakes.

And I am sitting in a bush.

11:56 p.m.

Oh yet more marvelous, marvelous news, the

Blunderboys are lurking around in the park. Probably setting fire to themselves and practicing being crap. Which they needn't bother doing as they are top at it anyway.

They'll sense I'm here in a minute and come looming out at me. The Blunderboys have got radar for girls within half a mile.

thirty seconds later

Mark Big Gob (who lives in my street and who I accidentally snogged once, and who has the largest lips known to humanity) larged out of the gloom and saw me panting in the hedge. He was looking at my nungas, which were heaving up and down. Stop heaving and retreat into your over-the-shoulder boulder holder, you stupid nungas! Mark said, "I see you are all pleased to see me, girls."

How repellent is he? I ignored him and got up with a dignity at all times sort of attitude. As I was brushing past him, he said, "Steady darlin', you nearly knocked me over, then."

The rest of the trainee idiots had sidled up by then and they sniggered and choked on their fags. Still, on the bright side cigarettes stunt your growth, so with a bit of luck most of them will

4

remain about three-foot eight.

Mark Big Gob said, "I see you've got the Horn. Is it for me?"

Is he mad? Is he implying that I have got the Horn for him? I would rather plunge my head into a bucket of whelks than let him anywhere near me. I can't believe that his hand had once rested on my basooma. And that his enormous gob had squelched around my face. Erlack. If anything, he gave me the anti-Horn.

Sadly, it was then I realized that in fact he was right, I did have the Horn. Horns actually. I was still carrying my Viking bison horns that I had worn to rehearse Rosie's wedding dance.

Still, what is so very unusual about that?

five minutes later

Quite a lot, actually, when you think about it.

Which I won't.

Oh double *merde* and *ordure* and poo.

12:15 p.m.

Got to my street. My tootsies are killing me. The light is still on in the front room. Oh noooo. That means the terminally insane (Mutti and Vati) are still up. I must avoid them at all costs. I can't speak to them. Not now. Not anytime if I have my way.

I snuck really really quietly through the front door and stashed my horns in a secret place where they will never be found (the ironing basket).

Aaahh. Safely in. Now quietly, quietly up the stairs to my room. Quietly, quietly like a little mousie. Mousie girl opening little doorsies. Shhhhh. Shhhh. Nearly safe. Quietly into the room like a quiet thing on quiet tablets. No sign of the furry freak brothers, a.k.a. my cats Angus and his cross-eyed son Gordon, thank the Lord.

As I opened my bedroom door Gordy's face appeared upside down an inch away from my fringe. I looked into his mad cross-eyes. Why does he do that—lurk on top of the door like a bat? He did a little croaky noise and licked my face with his horrid rough tongue. I managed not to cry out or be sick.

12:25 a.m.
There is a half-eaten mouse on my pillow.

12:30 a.m.
Oh God that means that Gordy licked my face

after he had crunched up the mousey head. I am almost bound to get the Black Death.

Nothing nicer than a few pustulating boils when you have boyfriend trouble.

one minute later

Crept downstairs to get rid of the mousey. I had it on a piece of cardboard. When I say mousey, what I mean is two ears and a bit of tail. Too crunchy for Gordy's delicate little murderer's gob, I suppose.

As I was going back upstairs, Mutti called out from the front room, "Is that you, Gee?"

I said, "No," and went up to get into my snuggly bed of pain.

one minute later

In bed under the sheets of life. Can't be bothered getting undressed as I'm so full of confusiosity.

five minutes later

I'd better make an effort though and at least take my boots off. My feet are probably all swollen from my mad running and I don't want to have them surgically removed again.

(The boots, I mean, not my feet.)

Anyway, the nub and gist is that I have accidentally acquired two Luuurve Gods.

I may never sleep again.

one minute later

I won't have time to sleep if I've got two boyfriends.

Teeheeee . . . Zzzzzzzzzzzzzzzzzzzzzzzzzzzz.

sunday july 17th
7:00 a.m.

Woke up from a dream where Dr. Clooney was looking at my head and saying, "I have never seen anything like it, her head is one enormous boil!" and for a minute forgot that I had two boyfriends.

I checked in the mirror and there has been no pustulating boil extravaganza, so I seem to have escaped catching the Black Death from Gordy's little mousey snack, thank the Lord. Although my head seems to have exploded, hairwise. I may have to iron it.

7:35 a.m.

Crept downstairs and made some toast and tea. I must keep my strength up. There was snoring coming from every room. Mum had made Dad sleep in the spare room because of his snoring and she was louder than him! I must be kind, though, she probably has difficulty breathing because of the weight of her enormous nungas. If mine grow as big as hers, I will definitely donate them to some charity.

It was a nice day. The birds were humming and the bees a-singing and I could see Angus the furry Luuurve Machine lolling around in the morning sun with Naomi. They are very much in love if the amount of bum-oley licking is anything to go by.

five minutes later
Back in my bed with snacksies.

I must consult with a book of wisdomosity.

five minutes later
This double boyfriend fandango is not mentioned in Mutti's book *How to Make Any Twit Fall in Love with You*.

three minutes later
Maybe Robbie and Masimo will have to have fisticuffs at dawn to decide who gets me. Who

knows what the right etiquette is in this scenario.

one minute later

One thing is for sure. I will not be asking Dave the Laugh, my Horn Adviser and occasional snoggee, to the fight. He will only think it is a laugh and start shouting out stuff like, "Hit him with your handbag, Masimo," or "Mind the hair, love."

Anyway, Dave is too busy to give me advice these days. He will be with his "girlfriend."

I wonder—what number they have got up to on the snogging scale?

Shut up, brain! I don't want to think about Dave—he is an ex-snoggee. And just a mate. I have enough to worry about without Dave popping up all the time—oo-er.

7:55 a.m.

This does mean that I am going to have to be on high beauty and glamorosity alert at all times. One of my multi boyfriends may be so driven by snognosity that he rushes round here first thing in the morning. I must be prepared. But no one must know. I must exude glamour but in a natural just-tumbled-out-of-bed way.

Soooo just a hint of foundation, touch of bronzer, lippy, mascara and tiny bit of eyeliner. Which I like to think looks like I have a touch of the Egyptian in my genes.

That is what I like to think.

8:00 a.m.
Now what to wear?

Nightwear or daywear?

What would you wear if you had unexpectedly woken up to the doorbell ringing and you didn't know who it was, but you suspected it might be a Luuurve or a Sex God?

8:01 a.m.
Not Teletubbies pajamas, that is *le* fact.

8:06 a.m.
A leatherette skirt and T-shirt that exude casualosity?

Yep.

8:12 a.m.
I took a peek out of the front window. No sign of any Sex or Luuurve Gods. The reverse, in fact,

because I was alarmed to see Mr. Across the Road in his garden in a shortie dressing gown. I hope he is not going to become a homosexualist in his twilight years. Then Mrs. Across the Road came out in a massive pair of pajamas. Was there the suggestion of a small mustache on her upper lip? Maybe that's what happens in the end when people are married: They change sex. My dad is certainly on the turn, but on the other hand no man alive has developed nunga-nungas like Mum.

8:30 a.m.
Why hasn't Jas phoned?

You would think that Radio Jas would have been on the airwaves of life wanting to know what happened to me and also wanting to report what had happened after I had left the gig. I suppose I will just have to wait until she wakes up, or the rest of the ace gang wake up to let me know what is going on. I must use the steely discipline for which I am world renowned.

8:35 a.m.
That's it, I can't stand it anymore. Crept out of the house. I won't leave a note because no one will

notice I am missing for hours. The last thing I want is a cross-examination from Herr Vati. Or Mum being "interested."

outside on the drive
Angus was still lying on his back on the wall whilst Naomi licked his face and then started in on his bum-oley. How disgusting. Kittyporn first thing in the morning.

Also, they are both covered in what looks like snot.

Oh, Blimey O'Reilly's trousers, it isn't snot; it's frogspawn. They have been maurauding about in Mr. and Mrs. Next Door's new marine conservation area. Known to other normal people as a bucket with disgusting tadpoles and slime and so on in it. The Prat brothers, also known as Mr. Next Door's annoying and useless toy poodles, were on marine conservation life-guard duty, so all Angus had to do was duff them up a bit, round them up into their kennel, and then it was a night of splashing around in the bucket to his heart's content.

The Next Doors will go absolutely ballistic; they always do about the least thing. Mr. Next Door has been hovering on the edge of a nervy spaz for the last year and this might drive him over the edge and into the rest home. His shorts will probably explode with the tension. Which is no bad thing, unless I happen to be around at the time and am exposed to the sight of his huge bottom looming about.

I said to Angus, "You are soooo bad, Angus, and in for big trub. That is a fact. *Au revoir*, dead kitty pal."

I'm sure he understands every word I say because he got idly to his feet, stretched and nudged Naomi off the wall. He treats his girls rough. Naomi leapt back on the wall and arched her back and raised her hackles, making that really mad screechy noise that Burmese cats do. She was spitting at Angus and teetering backward and forward. Really, really mad. Angus was frightened. Not. When she got near enough, he biffed her with his paw and she disappeared over the wall again. You had to laugh.

Not for long, though, because after he had rolled about on the lawn to get rid of the frogspawn, he began stalking me.

Oh no, not today, my furry friend, I am not having him tagging along with me all day causing mayhem and eating anything that moves. I said,

"Clear off, Angus, stay there. Sit. Sit."

I even threw him a stick to distract him and he ran bounding off after it, but then came back to trail along behind me.

I started running. He started running. I hid behind a wall. His head loomed over the wall at me.

In the end, to give him the hint, I threw stones at him—some of them quite big.

five minutes later
This is hopeless.

He doesn't care about having stones thrown at him at all. He is senselessly brave.

one minute later
He is trying to catch the stones in his mouth.

one minute later
He's just slightly dazed himself by heading one of them.

in jas's garden
9:00 a.m.
No sign of Jas being up and her curtains are drawn. Damny damn damn. She is so lazy, snoozing in

Pantsland. I don't want to arouse any interest in the elderly mad by ringing the bell. Even though Jas's m and d are on the whole more acceptable than most in that they provide snacks and Jas's dad doesn't speak, they are still technically in the elderly loon category.

three minutes later
How can I get Jas to get up without ringing the doorbell?

one minute later
Oh here we are! There is a ladder in the shed, I can use my initiative and Girl Guide training (which I haven't got and never will have) and use the ladder to make a small fire to send smoke signals past her bedroom window. Shut up, brain.

five minutes later
It must be a child's ladder, as it only reaches to just above the lounge window. I would have to have orangutan arms on stilts to reach Jas's window. Poo and *merde*.

two minutes later
As I was looking up wondering how to make my

arms grow, something bit my ankle really viciously. Angus was on the ladder with me, looking at me and playfully biting my legs. Ouch, bloody ouch.

I reached down to strangle him and I was just saying, "You bloody furry freak, I'll kill you when I get down from here" when I saw Jas's dad standing on the garden path with his paper, smoking his unlit pipe. He was looking at me. Like I was Norma Normal.

I said, "Aah yes, I was just . . . thinking I'd see what your garden looked like from up here. And yep, yep, it looks very, very nice indeed. Full of stuff. Growing and so on."

What am I talking about?

five minutes later

Jas's dad is sensationally nice, or insane, it's hard to tell. He let Angus carry his newspaper into the house, and didn't even seem to mind when he ate it.

in jas's bedroom

I managed to dig Jas out from underneath her owls. How many stuffed owls can one person collect? A LOT is the answer in her case. What is the matter with her? Also, she was vair vair grumpy when I woke her up with a kiss. It was only on her cheek, but you would think she had been attacked by hordes of lesbians in cowboy outfits. Blimey. She looks very odd in the mornings and her fringe was akimbo to the max. She looked like a startled earwig in jimjams.

I said, "So, so? What happened?"

She looked at me and started early morning fiddling with her fringe. Vair annoying.

She said, "You just ran off like a fool."

I said, "Yes, I know, I was there."

"Yes, you say that, but you weren't there, that is the whole point. And everyone was going, 'What's Georgia doing, has she gone mad?' and so on."

"Jas, if I get you a little cup of tea and a snacklet, will you try to be normal and tell me everything that happened? It is a matter of life and death. YOUR life and YOUR death."

ten minutes later

It's quite nice and cozy tucked up in bed with Jas and snacksies. Except that I think I have an owl's beak up my bum-oley. Jas was munching and rambling.

"Well, first of all, after you had run off like a ninny. By the way, you run in a really weird way in those high heels. You looked like Nauseating P. Green when she's playing hockey. Her legs go all spazzy and—"

I hit her with snowy owl.

She almost choked on her toast.

I said, "Jas, get on with it, I have only got about fifty more years to live."

"Well, first of all, the boys did that boy thing with Robbie."

"What boy thing?"

"You know, slapping each other on the shoulders, shaking hands and so on."

"Yeah."

Jas went on, "Robbie was saying hello to a lot of people and Masimo got his jacket on. You were just approaching the park by then, we could still see you. Masimo said to Tom, 'She asked me about footie results. Then she ran away. Is she normal?'"

Ohmygiddygod. I said to Jas, "What did Tom say?"

"Well he stood up for you, of course."

"I love Hunky very much, as you know, Jazzy Spazzy."

"Yes, he said you were quite often normal. He had seen you being normal once or twice himself. Usually when you were asleep."

Marvelous.

Apparently after I had run off to "catch my train," Masimo had gone home with the band, and just after he'd gone, Wet Lindsay had come stropping back looking for him. Jas said her no forehead was all crinkly and mad and her hair extensions were swishing around in a nervy b. central way. Then she had seen Robbie and was all over him like a rash and they had gone off together.

What, what???

I said, "Wet Lindsay went off with the Sex God?"

"Well, they did go out together once, didn't they?"

"Yes, Jas, I know, I was heartbroken. Do you remember? "

"I mean, maybe he still likes her, I don't know, maybe he has had a secret thing for her, some people like lanky girls."

"Jas, shut up now."

"Well, I am just saying that absence makes the heart grow fonder and so on. It's an ill wind that—"

"Jas, that is not shutting up, that is rambling on and on about rubbish."

She was chomping away on her Jammy Dodger like Wise Mabel of the Forest. I really, really wanted to shove it down her throat, but I knew it would take another million years to get the end of the story if I did, so I just said, "Jas, you know when you were going on and on about 'maybe something good will happen,' and I didn't want to go to the gig in the first place, but you persuaded me, well, did you know that Robbie was going to be there?"

"Well, I sort of thought he might. I knew he was coming home because he rang Tom and said that he had booked his ticket. And that he would be back in time for the gig."

"But did he say why he was coming home?"

"Erm, no, not exactly no."

Oh noooooo. I have left the cakeshop of luuurve thinking I have accidentally bought two cakes and found out that I may have only got one cake. And I might have already eaten that. I may in fact be cakeless.

I said to Jas, "We must call an emergency ace gang meeting."

"Well, I thought I might go to the river with Tom and—"

"No, Jas, you thought wrong."

park

midday

Angus is still trailing me around like Inspector Morse in a furry coat. (And on all fours.)

on the swings

Rosie said, "I hope this is worth it, Sven and me were going to practice artificial respiration on each other in case anyone chokes on the vats of mead at our wedding."

Even the ace gang has no sense of community these days. Jas bleating on about missing Tom, Jools wanting to go hang around Rollo whilst he played footie, Rosie banging on about Sven, half reindeer half fool, and Ellen . . . well, Ellen just being Ellen.

five minutes later

Ellen, Rosie, Jools, Mabs, Jas and me are all swinging on the swings. Not backward and forward like normal people enjoying a day in the park, but sideways so that the Blunderboys can't see anything. Life is not easy. The Blunderboys are in the bushes watching us on the swings. They think we don't know they are there; it's pathetic. They are so noisy and keep falling over things and fighting with each other.

five minutes later
Now the Blunderboys are lying down on the ground, hoping they might see up our skirts. I can see their beaky eyes blinking under the branches. If they do happen to see our knickers, they will think we are doing it on purpose to attract them. Dear God.

one minute later
Just then a Pekingese dog came hurtling by, dragging its lead behind it, followed by Angus. Oh no. He loves Pekingese. A LOT. I hope it is a fast runner.

Anyway, I haven't got the time to worry about everything. If careless people will let their small dogs loll around in parks they are asking for trouble. It's a cat-eat-dog world.

twenty minutes later

The general mood of the gang is that I should play it cool until I know what is really going on. Although what Ellen knows about cool I really don't know. She had a massive ditherspaz trying to describe how Dave the Laugh had said good night to her at the Stiff Dylans gig. Apparently, and I know this because I heard it about a zillion times, "Er. Well, then he well, and I didn't know, what, he meant, but then well he just said . . . he just said to me . . . he said . . ."

I shouted, "WHAT, what in the name of heaven, Ellen, WHAT, WHAT did he say?"

And I didn't even want to know, I just wanted to get to the bits about what happened after I left and what did people say about me and so on, but you know what people are like, it's just me, me, me with them.

Ellen went even more divvyish. Good grief.

"He said, 'Well good night then, Ellen, never eat anything bigger than your head.'"

I didn't know what to say.

No one did.

fifteen minutes later

Anyway, the nub and the gist is that the ace gang are useless and don't know anything more than I do. It seems they all watched me run off like a loon (to catch my train) and then lolloped home. Useless.

However, I decided to forgive them.

They are, after all, my besties.

And if I don't forgive them I will never find out anything. And also never go out again, and stay in my house with my parents.

So, grasping the bull by its whatsits, I said to the gang, "In order to make a full and frank decision boyfriendwise, I have to know the intentions of the prospective snoggees."

Ellen said, "Er, what are they, I mean who, what is, like a snoggee?"

"Ellen, keep up, the pro snogs are Masimo and Robbie. Masimo said that he was single and free for me, but on the other hand did not come running after me and stop me getting on my train. And Robbie only had time to say hello and then not long after went off with Wet Lindsay. Soooo, did Robbie come to the gig to see me, or does he just want to be friends with me? Why has he come home?"

Rosie said, "Someone must go underground and subtly find out what Robbie's intentions are. Shall I ask Sven? He could wear his camouflage flares."

I said, "No."

Jools said, "What about asking Dave the Laugh to find out?"

Ellen nearly fell over with pleasure. "Oh yes, well I mean, I could, well maybe I could like, go with him or something. Be like his assistant? But maybe that would be like too forward or some- thing. What do you think, or something?"

I said, "No, Ellen, it has to be this year, really."

Jas had gone off into Jasland. She was fid- dling with her fringe and I could tell she had Tom and voles on her mind.

I said, "There is someone here, isn't there, who knows Robbie's brother quite well, shall we say, and who could use subtlety and casualosity to find out stuff. Isn't there, Jas?"

Jas looked up like a dog when she heard her own name. "What do you mean, what do you want me to do?"

"I want you to find out about Robbie by asking Tom a few casual questions."

Jas said, "Oh OK. Can we go now?"

"The key word here, Jas, is 'casualosity.' Casualosity. Can you say that, Jas?"

Jas got into her huffmobile.

"I know how to be casual, Georgia."

"Wrong."

5:00 p.m.
In bed. I am absolutely full of exhaustosity. How difficult can it be to be casual? Four hours we have been coaching Jas. It was like talking to a lemming in a skirt.

First of all, we tried it her way. Always a mistake, in my humble (but right) opinion. Her idea of casualosity essentially means that she says: "Does Robbie fancy Georgia? Or is he normal?"

I had to use clevernosity to get Jas to do what I wanted in the end. I said, "I've got an idea, you know how good you were as Lady MacUseless and everything, Jas?"

Jas said,"Yes, it took quite a lot out of me, actually. Do you remember the bit when I had the dagger and . . ."

Oh no, three million years were going to go by whilst she relived her big moments in the school play.

I interrupted her by hugging her so hard that her head was buried in my armpit and said, "Yes, yes, now this is my idea."

I asked her to act out what she was going to do in an improvised scene like in drama. She loves that sort of thing, as she is such a teacher's bumoley kisser.

Rosie volunteered to be Tom. She said, "I've got the legs for it."

Incidentally I'm a bit worried that she was able to whip out a false beard from her rucky. I said that to her, I said, "Rosie, do you carry a beard around with you at all times?"

And she said, "Well, you never know."

The Viking bride to be gets madder and madder. We are definitely entering the Valley of the Unwell. Anyway Jas was mincing around like a mincing thing, warming up. Flicking her fringe at Tom (or Rosie in a beard, as we know him). It was incredibly irritating. I was on the edge of a mega nervy b. and supertizz as it was. I said, "Jas, what in the name of arse are you doing?"

And she said huffily, "I am getting into character."

I said, "But you are being you."

She looked at me like I had fallen out of her nose.

"I am finding the inner me."

Good grief. Her "inner me" is bound to be an owl.

Eventually she was ready and came pratting girlishly up to Rosie and twittered, "Oh Tom, I found some vole spore down by the woods."

Tom/Rosie said (in a French accent, for no apparent reason . . . it must be the beard), "Ah, did you, my liddle pussycat? Would you like to, how you say, kiss my beard?"

Jas actually blushed and said, "Well, you know I would, Tom . . . but maybe, you know, in private, not in front of everyone."

I had to put a stop to this, it was like watching some pervy film, like *Two Go Mad in Bearded Lezzie Land*. I said, "Will you get on with it!"

Jas predictably lost her rag immediately over the slightest thing and said, "I was just getting in the mood, actually, and anyway this is stupid, practicing to be casual, I know how to be casual."

I said, "Well, why don't you BE casual then?"

She gave me her worst look, but eventually after Mabs gave her a midget gem they started again.

Jas said to Rosie, who now had a pipe, "Tommy-wommy."

"Oui."

"Well, I was just, you know, thinking about Robbie, it's nice he's back, isn't it?"

"Mais oui—très très magnifique."

It was pointless objecting about the Froggyland language, especially as Ro Ro was now plaiting her beard.

Jassy said, "Did he come back, you know, because he missed England and his mates? Do you think he will join the Stiff Dylans again?"

I looked at Jas in amazement. She had asked an almost good question in a quite subtle way and not mentioned me. Blimey.

And it only took four-and-a-half hours of torture. We had to leave it there because Sven came along yodeling through the trees (no, I am not kidding).

5:30 p.m.

When would be a good time to call Radio Jas? Surely she must have had time to talk to Tom by now? I should exercise discipline and patience, of course.

5:31 p.m.

Phoned Jas.

"Jas."

"What?"

"It's me."

"Oh well, this is me, too."

"Jas, don't start."

"I'm not."

"Well, don't."

"Well, I won't."

"Good."

And I put the phone down. That will teach her.

two minutes later

"Jas, what have you found out?"

"I've found out that I am having scrambly eggs for tea. Byeeee."

And she put the phone down.

Damn.

I have my pride, thank goodness, no one can take that away from me. I won't be bothering Jas again, not whilst she is so busy stuffing her gob with eggy.

6:00 p.m.
This is torture, but I will never give in. Never, never. The Eggy One will never get the better of me.

6:10 p.m.
Phoned Rosie. I'll get her to phone Eggy and casually ask her, but not on my behalf.

6:20 p.m.
Rosie is out with Sven at the "pictures," her mum says. Oh yeah, as if. And the film they are watching is *Number Seven on the Snogging Scale.*

I daren't ask Ellen, Jools or Mabs to phone Jas, as they are bound to spill the beans to Eggy. The tragedy is that all three of them are such crap liars, it's a curse, really.

7:30 p.m.
She is soooooo annoying, she will never phone me if she has got the hump.

7:35 p.m.

Masimo hasn't called or anything. Maybe he really does think I am insane. Or maybe he thinks I caught the train from the shopping mall and have gone away for a few days. In which case he is insane.

If I have an early night I can do skin care, cleanse and tone and get everything ready for tomorrow just in case I have a chance encounter with one of my many maybe boyfriends on the way to Stalag 14.

8:15 p.m.

Blimey, I look about two and a half, I am so shiny-faced and clean. Also, I am nice and baldy everywhere, except on my head, of course, I do not want to have an Uncle Eddie hairstyle.

Actually my hair is a bit of a boring color. It hasn't got *je ne sais quoi* and umph.

bathroom
five minutes later

Ahaha, Mum has got some hair dye. Warm chocolate. That would be nice and groovy. I could just put a couple of streaks in the front, like highlights, or is it lowlights . . . hi-lo-it lights anyway, which is all that counts.

Got the dye and went into the front room. Oh how I wish I hadn't. Mum and Dad were all over each other on the sofa watching some old film with crying in it and blokes in tights and an Uncle Eddie bloke in a frock. Mum said, "Come and watch *Robin Hood*, it's good."

I said, "Mum, I'm just going to use your hair dye for a bit."

"No."

"Er, Mum, I think you are being a bit negative."

"No."

"But I—"

"No."

"Look at the color of my hair, it's crap. I might as well be the Invisible Mouse."

"No."

"But I . . ."

Then Vati joined in.

"Georgia, no, no, no and thrice no. And also no."

"Vati, I am not asking you, actually, I am asking my dear dear mum about her hair dye."

"It's not her hair dye, it's mine."

What??? What fresh hell? HIS hair dye? My

Vati, not content with growing small badgers on his chin and wearing leather trousers and having a clown car, was now trying to be Lady Cliff Richard. Or Lady Paul McCartney.

"Please say you are not serious."

Vati said, "I am very serious, I am a man in his prime, as your mother knows."

And he did that disgusting thing of grabbing one of her nungas, squeezing it and going, "Honk honk!!!"

Mum didn't even hit him, she just went all girlie and said, "Stop it, you big boy."

Vati was still in Madland, however, and said, "Yes, I thought I'd get down with the youth, you know, dye my hair, get the old leathers on and maybe check out a few clubs. Which one would you recommend?"

I nearly fainted.

Imagine bumping into my dad and his sad mates down at the Buddha Lounge!!!

Any chance I had of having a Sex God or a Luuurve God or even Spotty Norman would be well and truly up the pictures without a paddle. My dad's impression of Mick Jagger dancing could reduce people to tears, and not of admiration.

in the kitchen
9:00 p.m.

I must have toast to calm down.

I was buttering it when my mad little sister Libby popped her head out of the airing cupboard.

"Heggo, Ginger. Come in my nest. Now."

I looked up at her.

"Libbs, I'm too big for it."

"No."

"Yes, I am."

Her face went all frowny and she started snorting and tutting like she has heard Mum do. I wasn't liking this. The frowny face is not one I like to see because usually I am in agonizing pain seconds later.

However, this time it wasn't my turn to suffer. Libby disappeared into her "nest" and then Scuba-diving Barbie came flying out, quickly followed by Mr. Potato, Pantalitzer doll (well, the head) and finally, after a lot of panting and heaving and squealing, Gordy came hurtling through the air. He came to a skidding halt on the dish rack and then did that shivering thing before he hurled himself through the catflap.

Libby popped her head out again and smiled

in a terrifying way.

"Come on, Gingey . . . it's naaaaaice."

Oh dear, God. Still, what else was I doing this fine evening that I couldn't squeeze into an airing cupboard with my clearly insane sister? She looked me straight in the eye and said, "I lobe you VELLY times twice."

Aahhh. At least she "lobes" me, unlike my so-called bestie Jas. Who is dead girl to me now that she can't even perform the slightest task.

five minutes later

Sitting in the dark little cupboard, I had to bend double with my knees practically up my nose. Libby had snacks in there, which was nice—if you like bits of banana covered in fluff.

11:00 p.m.

Libby was only persuaded out of her "nest" by Mum saying she could sleep in my bed. Thanks, Mum.

For a little girl, Bibbs is very full of gas. Her farts are like gunshots and sooo smelly. If anyone lit a match, we would all be blown to kingdom come. And back. And there would still be some fart left over to cook on for the rest of the year.

11:20 p.m.

And the snoring. It's like comedy snoring except that I'm not laughing.

11:25 p.m.

Tried to shove Libby over onto her side to stop her snoring and got a smack around the head for my trouble. She is even violent when she is unconscious.

11:30 p.m.

I wonder what Robbie really came home for? I can't believe it was to see Wet Lindsay, surely Tom would have told me if he knew that Robbie fancied her. I bet she has been writing to him, pretending to be a nice person. How could he fancy her? Still, facts have to be faced, he did actually go out with her once before he started seeing me. And they must have been doing something in those months. They weren't talking about her ludicrous forehead.

He must have snogged her. If he went out with her for three months that is a lot of snogging opportunities. And she is bound to have been puckering up pretty nonstop because she has no pridenosity. I wonder—what number on the snogging scale they got to?

five minutes later
Clearly not No. 7 (upper-body fondling), otherwise her false nungas would have made a surprise appearance. Maybe that is what happened!!!
I wish.
Anyway, I don't want her nungas in my head.
Get out.

two minutes later
Does he like me or not?

one minute later
Do I like him or not?

11:40 p.m.
Hang on a minute, I've just realized something. I am on the rack of love again. How did this happen?
Well, I'm not dangling about up here anymore. I say no no no and thrice no to the rack. I am a free

woman. That woman Emily Plankton chained herself to a policeman and chucked herself under a horse and so on so that I could vote. I must not let her down.

11:50 p.m.
Although it does seem a bit over the top to chuck yourself in front of a horse so that you get to vote.

one minute later
Especially as, in fact, she was dead, so she couldn't vote anyway.

two minutes later
And neither can I.
    Like I have always said, history is crap.

midnight
On the other foot, Masimo said, "Now I is free man."
    And that means he wants to go out with me. So that is that. I have been to the bakery of love and I have got an Italian cakey.

five minutes later
But I might also have an éclair called Robbie, in

case I'm peckish and the Italian cakey isn't filling enough.

five minutes later
Some people, naming no names, but Jas, will probably say I'm greedy, but I'm not, I am just having a choice. I am not sad like Jas, who only stays with one boyfriend because she has no special talents. Other than an unerring eye for a crap owl, or being able to spot a vole at a hundred yards. Or having the largest knicker collection in the Northern Hemisphere. And being the biggest and most annoying twit on the planet.

two minutes later
Yes, the Good Lord has been kind enough to give me a couple of special gifts.

one minute later
Oh that was a bit freaky-deaky, I had Dave the Laugh's voice in my head when I said "a couple of special gifts." And his voice said, "Ah, yes . . . the nunga-nungas." He is even rude when I make him up in my head. That is very rude, indeed. It is rudey-dudey in absentia, as we say in Latin.

Every time I think about Dave the Laugh, it makes me laugh.

I've just remembered him (accidentally) switching all the lights off during *MacUseless* and the entire Forest of Dunsinane falling off the stage. God, it was funny.

one minute later
And his vair amusing "pant" thing—as in the famous song "The Hills Are Alive with the Sound of PANTS."

two minutes later
And when he put a FOR SALE sign on his school's roof—tee hee hee.

one minute later
Oy, shut up, brain! This is a Dave-the-Laugh-free zone!

five minutes later
If I do decide on the Luuurve God, it will serve Robbie right. He will just have to check into Heartbreak Hotel, like I had to when he dumped me. He should ask for the sobbing suite.

12:30 a.m.

I have never had to check in to Heartbreak Hotel because of the Luuurve God. Except, I suppose, I thought I might have to make a booking when he said he would tell me in a week's time if he was going to be my one and only one.

12:40 a.m.

But that was then, and now he has said, "I am for you if you want." Which is vair vair good.

12:45 a.m.

Good night, Luuurve God.

12:50 a.m.

I hope he doesn't think it's odd that I had to catch a train from near the shopping center.

At midnight.

When there wasn't a train station there.

1:00 a.m.

To be fair, I haven't really given Robbie much of a chance. Maybe I should at least talk to him before I, you know, choose my cake.

1:10 a.m.

I don't suppose they would both consider a time-share girlfriend. . . .

ZZZZzzzzzzzzzzzzzz.

snot disco dancing

monday july 18th

8:00 a.m.

This is the first day of the rest of my life. So why is my hair sticking up like a cockerel?

8:10 a.m.

Mum caught me ironing my hair. God, she made a big deal out of it. It's probably the first time she has seen an iron.

Bloody hell, ramble on, why don't you?

She was all red-faced. "By the time you are twenty-five, your hair will be like nylon."

I said, "Mum, who cares what I look like at twenty-five? I will be in the twilight zone of life by then, like you."

If I hadn't used my athletic responses, I could have been quite badly injured by Mum's hairbrush. She is very unstable.

8:20 a.m.

Scavenging around in the kitchen for something to eat. Luckily a piece of toast popped out of the toaster. Ah, good. I buttered it and ate it. Blimey, being a Love Goddess can make you peckish.

Vati came dadding in. He didn't even say "Good morning." He said, "Is that my toast you are eating?"

I said, "To be honest, Dad, I don't think you need any more toast, you seem to have plenty stored away around the trouser area."

As usual in this house when anyone (me) tries to be light and amusing, Dad goes ballisticisimus. Mum came in trying to force Libby into her dungies whilst she still had a cup of milky pops in her hand which she would not let go of.

Dad was still moaning on about me. "Where does she get all this rudeness from, Connie? You are too easygoing on her."

Mum said, "I know, she's been ironing her hair."

Dad forgot about the toast fiasco and started on beauty. Something which quite frankly he is not an expert on.

"How bloody ridiculous is that? You'll end up like Uncle Eddie."

I said, "Oh right, I'm going to turn into a mad

bloke on a motorbike because I straighten my hair.
I think women everywhere should be told."

8:30 a.m.
I hate my parents. They are so unreasonably mad.

8:35 a.m.
And so self-obsessed. They don't seem to understand that their lives are over, and I am covered in
cake.

8:36 a.m.
I am nearly at Jas's house. I must exude calmnos-
ity and friendlinosity. I must put the egg incident
behind me and be nice to Jas, so she will tell me
all she knows.

8:40 a.m.
When I got to Jas's gate, it was to see her bottom
waggling off in the distance. Of course Eggy had
set off. She will still be having the huff with me. I
must be at my most charming. I did my fast walking until I caught up with her and gave her a lovely
smile as I linked arms with her.
  "Hello, Jas, my little chummly-wummly."

She shook me off. "Don't hang on to my arm, Georgia, I'm not dragging you up the hill to school just because you are tired."

"I'm not tired, I am just so glad to see you, you lovely big-pantied loon."

I chucked her under the chin, but she still wasn't having it. So I stopped and stood in front of her and looked into her eyes.

"Jazzy Spazzy, you know I love you."

She went all red. Some Foxwood lads who had been trailing us uselessly as usual shouted, "Oy you lezzies, won't she give you a kiss?"

And another one said, "Can we see your breasts, please?"

Good grief.

Jas started flicking her fringe like a mad thing.

"Now look what you've started."

We set off at a spanking space for Stalag 14. As we went along, I was doing my special pleading, it was very touching.

"Jas, please forgive me. Did you find out anything? I know you will have done, because you are so vair vair clever. And top girl at blodge and . . . er, everything."

As we took our coats to the cloakroom she

relented a bit. "Well, I did talk to Tom in a casual way, even though you said I couldn't."

"Jas, Jas, I knew you could do casualosity big time, don't forget I have seen you in your nighttime panties, relaxing and at play."

As the bell rang for Assembly I could see the Hitler Youth (prefects) approaching, keen to do a bit of poncing around like prats.

I said, "Please, pleasey please tell me what Tom said."

"Well he said . . ."

"Yes, yes."

"Well he said . . . he didn't know anything."

"Pardon?"

"Robbie is having a break from farming in Kiwi-a-gogo, but he doesn't know how long he is staying."

Is that Detective Inspector Jas of Scotland Yard's idea of finding out stuff?

I wanted to kick her in the shins, but just in the knickers of time I remembered that she is my best pally and I gave her my "interested" smile.

Jas was starting to say, "Yes, so I don't really know if he likes you or not," when Wet Lindsay slimed up alongside me with Astonishingly Dim

Monica as sidekick slug and weed.

Wet Lindsay's hair extensions have been redone, how vair vair chav and naff she is. Having longer hair only draws attention to her lack of forehead and general octopus tendencies.

I forced myself to look at Wet Lindsay's forehead as if Jas had told me a good joke about it and laugh merrily. Wet Lindsay said to me, "What have you got to laugh about, Nicolson? Have you caught sight of yourself in a mirror?"

Oh my aching sides!!! How I laughed. Not. Astonishingly Dim Monica did, though, sniggering and snorting like a fool on fool tablets. I just said, "How very natural your hair looks, Lindsay. It really suits you and brings out all your best features, especially your knees."

She went a bit red round the earlobes and said, "Prat."

Charming. Absolutely charming. I said to Jas as we went into the hall, "Charming, utterly utterly charming. Who wouldn't want to go out with her?"

ace gang headquarters
break
Rosie blew a bubble-gum bubble that exploded all

over her nose. Very amusing. She had a big blob hanging off her nose like a huge bogey.

She said, "Look how it dangles about. I bet I can swing it round and round in time to some music. Like a snot disco. You lot sing something jolly and I'll improvise on bogey work."

five minutes later
I think despite being slightly singed in the oven of luuurve, I may be going to die of laughing. The snot disco dance is officially born. Danced to the tune of *EastEnders*, it is, "Swing your snot to the left, swing to the right. Full turn, shoulder shrugging, now nod to the front, dangle dangle, hands on shoulders and kick kick to the right, dangle dangle, kick kick to the left, dangle dangle and then full snot around and shimmy to the ground."

Excellent in every way.

As we strolled back for an action-packed morning of being bored and depressed I said to the gang, "I bet we could have the snot coming out of our nostrils all during German and Herr Kamyer wouldn't notice. Or if he does, we could pretend we have really bad colds. Hand over the bubble gum, girls, and get chewing!"

german

It was a triumph, darling, a triumph!!! We were all translating from our textbooks—what larks! The Koch family were off on another camping trip, taking an enormous amount of food with them, as usual. In our books there are hilariously bad illustrations of the Koch family, drawn by a blind person. Mrs. Koch looks vair like Herr Kamyer in a frock. I never get tired of the Kochs. In fact, I am thinking of writing to the author of the textbook (A. Schmidt, no, I'm not joking), and asking where the Kochs live. I want to write a letter to them, thanking them for the endless hours of fun they have given us all.

I put up my hand to ask a pressing Koch question. When Herr Kamyer noticed my hand blowing in the wind he said, "*Jah*, Georgia?"

"Herr Kamyer, there is a strange-looking thing in one of the pictures of the Kochs. It looks like a very tiny poo on a plate. But that doesn't seem right."

Herr Kamyer blinked through his moley glasses. "Ah, bring up ze picture, Georgia, und we will see."

I quicky attached my bubble-gum bogey as I

pretended to sneeze into my hankie and went up to his desk with the snot rag still covering my nose.

Herr Kamyer didn't notice. He is so INTER-ESTED in things; it's tragic, really. He actually seems to believe that we want to learn things. I put the textbook down in front of him at the picture of the Kochs and pointed to the poo on a plate.

"Ach so, Georgia, *der spangleferkel* . . . oh *jah*, I remember ven as a youngen ve vent into the voods camping, we would cook up the *spanglefer-kel* and sing our songs around ze campfire. The fun ve had camping. You vould have loved it, girls."

I still had my hankie out to disguise the bogey, but when he started humming, "Gif me ze campfire light *und komt mit me* to *der liebe liebe Rhein*," and took his glasses off to clean them. Or perhaps he was crying. Who knows? Who cares? Anyway, when he did that, I took the opportunity to let the bogey run free and wild. I even did a bit of the bogey dance slightly behind him and managed to get the hankie back in place before he finished. When I walked back to my desk the whole class spontaneously clapped. Herr Kamyer thought it was for his crap camping song and bowed. Quite sensationally German.

five minutes later

Sadly, Herr Kamyer really thinks we love his camping stories. He's going on and on about what they did. How they sang songs and cooked over the campfire.

twenty minutes later

Swapping notes. Rosie wrote, "Dear fellow loons, Let us have a scoring system for bogey work. Gee gets 5 points for her excellent letting the bogey run free and wild over Herr Kamyer's head. Similar acts earn 5 points and the first to get to 20 gets free Jammy Dodgers for life. Well, for a bit, anyway. Ro Ro, advisor to the stars xxxxx."

Of course there is always a dog in the manger of life. Jas wrote back and said it was "silly" and "childish." Hilarous really, coming from someone who practically snogs owls. Ellen was dithering about. Even in her notes. She wrote, "Hi everyone, it's me. Erm, about the snot disco, well, you know, I don't know. Like, er, what if we er, get into er, like trouble? What do you think, or something?

Er . . . Ellen

xxx"

on our way to french

Jas and Ellen have formed their own little break-away gang and they are living in a snot-free zone. They should grow up.

french

Drat and dratty drat drat Rosie is catching up pointswise by letting her bogey dangle over Mme. Slack's head as Mme. Slack is checking her homework. We were all trying not to laugh and Mme. Slack must have sussed something because she unexpectedly looked up and nearly got the pretend bogey in her eye. As she was looking at Rosie, Rosie casually popped the "snot" into her mouth and started chewing.

Mme. Slack went ballisticisimus and Rosie has got detention.

4:10 p.m.

Home time for some. As we went by the hall we saw Rosie's face at the window. She pressed her nose against the pane of glass so that it spread out like a trapped piglet. Vair funny. She mouthed "I love you all," and then disappeared from view.

in my bedroom

6:00 p.m.

Lying on my bed. No phone calls or anything from any of my so-called maybe perhaps boyfriends. I'm all aloney on my owney. Even Dave never rings me these days, not even as a matey-type mate, which he is. And the Swiss Family Mad are out at some sad tea party, wrecking people's lives with their weird ideas and Dad's huge bottom.

6:30 p.m.

I may as well go to sleep early and get as much beauty sleep as I can. Just in case all my boyfriends come home to roost at once.

I wonder—what they are all doing?

Maybe I've imagined it all. Maybe Masimo didn't mean he wanted to be my one and only one. Maybe he just wanted a snog. Or maybe he thinks I still like Robbie and that's put him off. Maybe he's right—maybe I do still like Robbie. Maybe . . . I should just call him.

6:40 p.m.

Boom crash bang. Yowl yowl. Now what?

Then I heard the lovely tones of my father.

"Bloody hell, that furry bastard has stuck its claws into my arse."

How delightful my home life is. It's practically like living in *Pride and Prejudice* it's so elegant. I will pretend to be asleep. Not that anyone cares. I have asked them to respect my privacy, but I bet they—

Ah, yes. My door crashed open.

I said, "Mum, I am asleep, actually."

Mum said, "Don't you want your letter then?"

I sat up in bed. "What letter?"

She held out an envelope. "This one. It was on the doormat before you got home from school. I put it in my bag and forgot about it. It must have been hand delivered, because it's only got your name on it."

I said, "Quick, give it to me, it is a criminal offense to tamper with Her Maj's mail."

"Who do you think it's from?"

"Er, Father Christmas. Possibly someone from beyond the grave. Mum, I don't know because you have got it and I therefore have not opened it."

ten minutes later

At last she has gone. She hung about a bit hoping

I would let her know who it was from. Looking at my things, saying meaningless stuff like, "What is my black leather jacket doing in your wardrobe? And my Chanel bag?"

Utterly pointless things. Tutting and carrying on like a tutting thing in a tut shop. But I just looked at her until she left.

five minutes later

I am so nervy that I can't open the letter. My name is written in capitals so I can't even recognize the hadwriting. What if it is from Masimo to say that having seen me scamper off at high speed like a prat, he has decided he is not a free man for me? Or what if it is from Robbie, saying that he has always loved me and would I be his?

Or what if it is from Oscar, trainee Blunderboy, asking me on "a date" to go skateboarding? Or what if it is . . . Oh shut up, shut up.

two minutes later

When you are having a tizz in nervy b. central, Call-Me-Arnold the Vicar says you should always ask the question, "What would Baby Jesus do?"

one minute later

I don't know why, though, because clearly Jesus'
dad is like a huge owly-type person, beaking about
looking at everyone and everything, even when
they are on the loo. As Big G is omniPANTSient
and set the whole thing up in the first place, he
would know who had written the letter and what
was in the letter already, without having to open it.
Or send it, even. So what is the point of asking
what Baby Jesus would do? Actually, when you
think about it on the whole, life is a charade and a
sham. It's a bit like mime, isn't it? Why do we have
to guess what is going on, why can't Big G just tell
us and get it over with?

five minutes later

What if the note is from Masimo and it just says,
"Arrivederci."

Or from Robbie and it says, "Oy Georgia, stop
looning about after me, you are only embarrassing
yourself. I am deeply in love with a wombat that I
met in Kiwi-a-gogo land and will play my guitar in
rivers only for her. In fact I have written a song for
Gayleen (the wombat), which I enclose. It goes
"You are my marsupial, my only marsupial, you

make me happy when skies are gray, you'll never know, dear, how much I love you, please don't take your furry face away."

ten minutes later
I have never had what is known as great letters from Robbie, when you come to think about it. The first one he wrote me was to dump me and suggest I go out with Dave the Laugh.

two minutes later
I wish I could phone the Hornmeister up now. This is when his Horn advice would be really good. Things have been a bit weird between us since he started seeing Emma. She's so nice, it's depressing.

Maybe that's why he's going out with her— because she's so nice, he doesn't know how to dump her.

Or maybe he likes nice people. Even her hair is nice. And her nose. How annoying is that?

And she's nice to me.

I hate that.

ten minutes later
Perhaps I can sort of sense what the words say by

looking at the envelope and using my psychedelic powers. I saw some geezer in a frilly shirt on TV who said that we all could tap into our clairvoyant side if we just concentrated.

I am looking at the envelope and concentrating.

five minutes later
My eyes have gone all blurry. Oh excellent, I am going blind. That's perfect, isn't it? Now even if I open the letter, I won't know what it says or who it's from.

one minute later
I can see a bit now. However, I think this is a lesson for us all . . . never trust blokes who wear frilly shirts and they are not doing it for a laugh.

one minute later
OK, this is it. I am opening the letter.

7:40 p.m.
The letter said:

Hi Georgia,
Since you had to, er, catch your train last

Saturday I haven't been able to get to see you. Do you fancy going for a coffee tomorrow night? I'll meet you at the bottom of East Street at 7:30 p.m. and we can catch up. I promise not to bring any photos of sheep. Jas tells me that you are allergic to wildlife. . . .
Robbie

Blimey. I am still as full of confusiosity. Is this good or bad? Am I glad it is from Robbie? Why hasn't Masimo got in touch? What does Robbie mean by "going for a coffee"? That is as bad as "See you later" in boyspeak.

one minute later
Does "going for a coffee" mean, you know, "going for a coffee"? Or does it mean, "Let us start with coffee and end up at No. 7"?

I must phone Jas.

Jas's dad answered. Blimey. I'd never heard him speak on the phone before, I'd only seen him sucking on his pipe, reading his paper or going out in sensible welligogs. Which is what you want in a dad, pipe sucking, silence and going away, but can you tell my vati that? No, you can't.

Jas eventually came to the phone.

She said, "What?"

"Why did you say 'what' like that?"

"Like what?"

"Don't start, Jas, I have just had a letter from Robbie."

"Oh, did he dump you?"

"No."

"Really? Blimey. I thought he might have been put off by your running. It's really weird, you know."

"Well, he wasn't, and he wants me to go for a coffee."

"Blimey."

"I don't know what going for coffee means."

"Blimey."

"Jas, can you say something else besides 'blimey'?"

"Gee, I have to go now because Tom is leaving and I won't see him again for seventeen and a half hours."

Oh dear Gott in Himmel.

four minutes later

Back in bed trying to keep my mind on higher things.

I wonder what number Jas'n'Tom have got up to on the snogging scale.

I have been very lax about finding out.

For the sake of science I think I had better do a survey of the ace gang and see if anything needs to be added since ear nibbling.

ten minutes later

I don't know why I am bothered, though. There might as well not be a snogging scale as far as I am concerned. I am well and truly a snog-free zone, which is unusual when you are supposed to be a boy magnet and have two or more Luuuurve Gods in your handy pandies.

In fact, when was the last time I snogged anyone, man or beast? (Not counting accidental tonguesies with my sister.) I may have forgotten all my skills, which I had better polish up on in case I have to pucker up for the Sex God.

What is that ludicrous thing that Jazzy Spazzy does? Oh yes, pucker, relax, pucker, relax.

five minutes later

I am full of snogging practice exhaustosity.

two minutes later

I hope doing this puckering malarkey is not going to mean I end up looking like Mark Big Gob. I had better not overdo it; no one wants to go out with a whale.

When was the last time I snogged the Sex God? Also, where is the last letter he wrote to me from Kiwi-a-gogo land?

one minute later

Oh, I know, I hid it on the top of my wardrobe in the only snooper-free zone in my so-called room.

one minute later

Why would a cat eat a letter? Why? It can't be hunger. But if you start asking questions about cats, you'd end up with the rest of the loons in the twilight home. Why do they eat spiders, that would be another one. There is not much nutrition in a spider, is there? And also, Angus doesn't really eat them, he just lets them loll out of the corner of his mouth in a disgusting way.

two minutes later

I've managed to read bits of the chewed-up letter.

And also found my missing fountain pen. Also heavily chewed. Don't tell me Angus and Gordy are cowriting a book. *Cat Tips on How to Really Annoy Your Baldy Owners*.

1. Hide their things and chew them.
2. If you are soaking wet from the rain, here is a top tip: Leap into your owner's lap and get nice and dry there.
3. Sit on walls and just look at them.

five minutes later

The only sense I can make from Robbie's chewed-up letter is, "Tom told me about your excellent dancing to 'Three Little Boys'... and you are, in the nicest possible way, quite possibly clinically insane."

This does not give the impression of sophisticosity that I want.

8:20 p.m.

I think I will just play the special CD he recorded for me before he went to Kiwi-a-gogo, to get me back in the mood.

8:45 p.m.

I tell you what I will not be doing: I will not be

lying with my head in his lap whilst he sings "I'm not there" to me. I have just remembered doing that in the park the summer before he went away. And I could see right up his nose. If I had been looking. Which I wasn't because I had my eyes closed and was nodding my head along in time to the music.

two minutes later
I've just remembered something else. I had a lurking lurker. Oh brilliant, now I have thought about lurkers, I am almost bound to get one.

one minute later
I must not get stressed out, that is the kind of thing that lurkers love.
    I must be calm. Ohm.

three minutes later
Ah, my little furry letter-eating pals Angus and his adolescent son Gordy have come to keep me company in bed. That will be nice and soothing having them purring beside me. They seem in a nice sleepy mood for once. So night night, world.
    Sex Kitty signing off.

ten minutes later

Fat chance. Other people have pets and I've got the furry freak brothers. They've done the flattening the bed down, pacing round and round and now they are doing that really really irritating prodding with their paws, kneading me like a dough person.

I will be a hollow-eyed wraith at this rate if I don't get some beauty sleep. I must do some inner calming exercises. Ooohhhmmm ohmmmmm.

Ooooohhhhhmmmyyygod. Mum has slammed into my inner sanctum carrying the spawn of the devil in her nightime nappy and deelyboppers.

I said, "What? What is it you people want of me???"

Oh brilliant, Bibbs is being bunged into my bed with me because she won't go to sleep without me. I said to Mum, "Mum, I am sure there is some European law against this kind of overcrowding. Even in poor people's land, I bet they don't have as many people and stuff in bed with them as I do."

She just said, "Don't be silly, Gee, read Bibbsy a little boboland story."

Libby had a big book with her that she smashed me in the nose with in a loving way as she snuggled in, pushing Gordy out of bed. He had just nodded off and crashed to the floor. He went ballisticisimus, yowling and shivering and attacking the bedside light before leaping back onto the bed and burrowing up from the bottom. His head popped up in between the book and me and he spat at me. Good grief.

Libby said, "Aaaah naaaaice and comfy. Readey book, Ginger. About Sindyfellow. Now."

I am a slavey girl in this family of loons, furry or otherwise.

ten minutes later

Blimey O'Reilly, I thought that *Heidi* was boring, cheese and goats and old grumpy blokes for as far as the eye can see, but *Cinderella* takes the bloody bee's pajamas on the boring and depressing front. This is the story: Cinderella lives with her ugly stepsisters. They hate her because she is pretty, although I can't say I blame the uglies. Looking at the drawing of Cinders, I would be inclined to give her a bit of a duffing-up. She has a very irritating sticky-up nose.

I read the story as fast as I could to get it over with: "Cinders is doing cleaning cleaning, some poncey bloke in a wig invites the sisters to a ball, Cinderella can't go because she is in rags and then some bint turns up in wings and changes her frock into a ballgown and some cats and mice and a pumpkin into a coach and horses. Moaning Minnie (Cinders) dances with some other poncey bloke in a wig (not the first one), leaves at midnight, tries on a shoe and marries Prince Wiggy. The end."

Libby laughed like a loon the whole way through, I don't know why. I don't want to know why.

You see, this is the sort of story that irresponsible fools (my mutti) make their children read. No wonder they are all mad and covered in cat food like my sister is.

And of course the whole facsimile of a sham turned to violence because Libby wanted to change Angus into a horse like in the story and banged him with her "wand" (my tennis racket), and the rest is history. Well, the vase in the knitted coverlet that Grandad's girlfriend Maisie gave me is history, Angus leaped up (not exactly changed into a horse as such) onto the windowsill and careered about, scattering my CDs, photos and the vase all over the place.

How can I be expected to have a decent snog-ging relationship with anyone whilst my home life is so bonkers?

tuesday july 19th

stalag 14

I had to practically iron my face this morning. I had slept facedown because I was so exhausted from the nighttime shenanigins and ordure. My nose was flat like a plate, all across my head. I had to use hot flannels to smooth it into a reason-able(ish) state. The only positive thing is that we have German today so at least I will be able to do my premakeup makeup in peace.

in the cloakroom

Talking to Jassy about my letter from Robbie, I said, "How come you told Robbie that I hate wild-life?"

"You do."

"That is not the point, you should tell him something about my finer points, not ramble on about rubbish."

"What are your finer points?"

I may have to kill her, but I won't be able to do

it in Assembly because Hawkeye is on Seeing Eye dog duty this morning. She never seems to tire of hating us. I reckon she limbers up every morning at home, shouting, "I hate all girls, I hate them. What do I do? I hate them!!!"

fifteen minutes later

Oh for heaven sakes, why does Slim bother going on and on? What is she talking about now? Isn't it bad enough that we have to get up at the crack of eight o'clock, get dressed, turn up, hang around all day being bored and depressed and usually get detention for our trouble? But she wants to talk as well. Why? What can she possibly say that would . . . then I heard the dreaded words "Four A are going on an exciting field trip in the last week of term." What? What??? I looked at the ace gang and they looked at me. Slim went on, in tip-top jelloid mode. Her nungas were practically doing the Charleston. Separately. She said, "I think it's marvelous, and just shows the kind of spirit that we foster in this school. Herr Kamyer came up with the idea after form Four A expressed interest in the camping trips that he used to go on in the German forests. I am sure that this is a lovely surprise for all of Four

A. Instead of normal lessons next Friday you will go by school bus to the lovely Cow and Calf Valley and camp there overnight. There are printed details for you to take home to your parents. Round and about the site there is an absolute cornucopia of wildlife, riverlife abounds, and in the evenings Miss Wilson, who has volunteered to accompany Herr Kamyer, will be teaching you some of the games and songs that she was taught herself as a young lady. The whole thing sounds like a real treat. I only wish that I were able to come myself."

We were all absolutely speechless. Rosie pretended to faint, which I thought was very funny. Wet Lindsay came bustling over and said, "Get up, you twit." Rosie said, "Oh where am I? Am I in heaven? Are you Gabriel?"

Lindsay said, "Think how excited you will be if you get to help with gardening duties after school."

Rosie did actually make quite a startling recovery. She was saying, "Oh I feel much much better now after my little rest."

And Lindsay slimed off. How I hate her. It gives me energy, the amount that I hate her.

ace gang heaquarters
break

I am definitely beyond a shadow of a doubt not going on the camping trip. Not. Never and also NO.

I said that to the gang.

Jas said, "I think it will be really good fun."

I looked at her.

Rosie said, "I told Herr Kamyer that I will be having my period, because usually if you mention anything like that he has the ditherspaz to end all ditherspazzes and his head drops off with redness. But he just said, 'Ach, hmmm, vell pop along to see Mizz Vilson, she is in charge of the ladies' area of things.' And I couldn't discuss it with Miss Wilson, as she would probably tell me about what she does when she has a period and then I would die."

I said, "We must make a plan, perhaps we could all have a sort of accident."

Mabs said, "Like what?"

"Erm, we could fall in a hole."

Jools said, "What hole?"

I said, "Er, we could dig one."

Jools said, "We could dig a hole and then fall in it?"

"Yes."

Rosie said, "Excellent idea, Georgia, quite startlingly insane, even for you."

Ellen said, "It might, you know, it might like be, well you know . . . like, well . . ."

I said, "Crap?"

Ellen dithered on, "No, it might be like, quite a good laugh."

Alarmingly all of the ace gang didn't seem to mind the trip. They seemed to think it might be "a laugh."

five minutes later

We discussed the "coffee with Robbie" scenario.

Rosie said, "So he says he wants to 'catch up with you,' but he sent you a letter, so that means it's not like a casualosity sort of fandango because he would have just phoned you if it was, wouldn't he?"

I nodded and went, "Uh-huh, uh-huh. . . ."

Jools said, "When you meet him, let him say stuff. Don't you start talking rubbish first."

I nodded and went, "Uh-huh, uh-huh. . . ."

And Jas said, "Georgia, why are you doing an impression of one of those nodding dogs in a car?"

five minutes later

It's surprising how much relief from tensionosity you can get merely by giving Jas a Chinese burn.

3:00 p.m.

I have managed to take my mind off my "coffee" with Robbie by applying two coats of nail varnish and coloring in all the "o's" in my Charlie Dickens book *Crap Expectations.* There are many more than you think; it may well be a lifetime's work.

4:20 p.m.

As I skedaddled home, all the ace gang gave me the Klingon salute for luck. Jools said, "So is it Robbie you like, then?"

I said with great dignitosity, "He is on my list."

I thought I heard Jas say, "Tart." Which is unnecessary. And also at some time will cost her a quick plunge into the nearest ditch. Maybe if I am forced to go on the ridiculous camping fiasco, I can think of an amusing revenge involving twigs and her pants.

home

Anyway, I am going to get this camping thing out

of the way so that I can just concentrate on my love life.

I wonder why I still haven't heard anything from Masimo. It's been three whole days now. And no one seems to have seen him.

two minutes later
What does it say in the *How to Make Any Twit Fall in Love with You* book? I'm just going to open it randomly and see what it says.

one minute later
"Boys live mostly in their heads." What is that supposed to mean? I wouldn't live in my head, I can tell you that. It's full of rubbish.

one minute later
Ooohhh well, I can only think of one cake at a time, my hands are full (oo-er).

6:00 p.m.
What is the matter with my parents? They will not do the least thing for me. I simply asked my vati to send a letter saying that I could not go on the school trip to a field because we had planned to do

something as a family.

Vati said, "We haven't planned anything."

I said patiently, "I know that, Vati, it is merely a cunning ploy."

"You mean a lie."

"Yes, exactly . . . er, I mean, well, not really, you see what it is is that I am allergic to the country-side."

Vati, as usual when he is intellectually challenged, resorted to coarse and unnecessary language.

"You do talk absolute bollocks, Georgia."

That is a nice way to talk to a sensitive growing teenager, isn't it? No wonder my hair won't go right and I am almost constantly in detention. Then he walked out of the room. I followed him. Was he wearing hipster jeans or was it just that his bottom was growing?

I decided not to ask.

"Dad . . ."

"Georgia, you are going on the field trip. We can take Libby to Grandad's and then your mum and I can have some time to ourselves for once."

"Mum doesn't want time with you, you will only talk about rubbish and set fire to your farts and so on. Please please don't make me go. I may die in the forest eaten by voles."

"Good."

6:30 p.m.

God I am so tense. I've spent precious makeup sex-minxy time trying to talk some sense into my father and now I have only an hour to get ready for the Sex God. I must concentrate.

6:32 p.m.

How do I feel about meeting Robbie? I had eschewed him with a firm hand. And now he wants to shake my hand, and put my hand . . . Shut up about hands! Stop going on and on about hands!! Be a hands-free zone!!!

Oh brilliant news, my brain has popped off on an away day to Loonchester!

6:35 p.m.

I've put really loud music on to drown out my brain whilst I do my makeup. I wonder whether he will have a Kiwi-a-gogo accent. He will probably say "Gidday cobbler" or whatever it is they say.

I've got this stuff that you paint on your lipstick and it makes it stay on, even through snogging. I tried snogging my arm in a very passionate way and it remained lippy-free. So *resultio*!!!

one minute later
But I don't know why I'm bothered about snogging because I might just be drinking coffee.

I wonder if I put the stuff on my eyeliner it would stop it coming off as well. Sometimes when I go to the loo after dancing like a loon I look like Polly the Panda.

7:10 p.m.
Ow buggery bugger. It's like putting paint stripper on your eyelid.

Ow.

My eyes will probably all swell up now. I must keep them very wide open.

7:15 p.m.
I've got my blue leather skirt and black top on and my ankle boots. I might take a jacket just in case he wants to er . . . wander about in the woods or something.

My hands are shaking so much I can't do the buttons up.

I must be cool and calmy calm. I must not under any circumstances turn into ditherqueen and remind Robbie how much younger than him I am. I must exude sophisticosity at all times.

Nearly fell down the stairs because I was trying to keep my eyes open. Mum came out of the kitchen.

"Where are you going?"

"Just round to Jas's."

"What, with half a ton of makeup and your shortest skirt on?"

"Mum, just leave it for once. Remember when you were young, there must be some papyrus scroll somewhere that will remind you of what it was like."

She looked at me. "Georgia, that is not the way to get a favor out of me."

I would have to risk it. I said, "Mum. The letter was from Robbie. You know, from before? Well, he has come back unexpectedly and I don't know why, but he asked me to meet him tonight. Please don't ruin my life."

To my amazement she said, "Alright, but you must be back at a reasonable time, otherwise your dad will have one of his turns and no one wants that."

What? No argument? As she went off she said, "You look lovely. Why wouldn't he want to go out with you? Just try not to do that thing that you do when you are nervous and your brain drops out. And why are you staring at everything?"

I gave her a quick kiss and leapt out of the door.

ten minutes to get to east street
Pant pant.

five minutes later
Nearly there. I must stop my starey eyes now and prepare for sticky eye work like what it says in *How to Make Any Twit Fall in Love with You*. Yes and it is also time for hip work. And . . . hip swing, hip swing, flicky hair flicky hair, licky lips, hip swing, hip sw—

There he was! Robbie the Sex God. How many hours had I spent longing for this moment? How many times had I cried myself to sleep just dreaming of him coming to meet me?

He looked vair cool and tanned. Not in an English way, which is a bit like crispy bacon bits with a touch of tomato sauce, but in a groovy gravy sort of way. He was wearing all black. A suit with a collarless black shirt. My heart went all melty. And my legs. And my brain. Hurrah, jelloid girl was back! He turned round and saw me and smiled and shook his hair back out of his eyes. They were incredibly blue black against his tan and all softy looking and he looked like he really liked me. I held my hand out for him to shake. Why? Had I turned into the Duke of Edinburgh? He smiled in a puzzled sort of way but took my hand and shook it.

"Er, how do you do? You're not dashing off for a train, are you?"

I went beetroot.

"No, I—well, that was a bit of a misunderstanding, trainwise."

"What, you mean as there is no train station in town?"

"Yes, that will be the one."

He laughed then.

"I'd almost forgotten how interesting life can be around you, Georgia."

But he said it in a sort of nice way.

And I said, "Hgnnfff."

Which is a quite brilliant thing to reply if you

83

want someone to run away.

Robbie looked at me. "Look, let's just try and relax and have a nice time, it's OK. We haven't seen each other for ages."

two minutes later

He really is vair groovy looking. I had slight jelloid knickers. Then I heard Jas's voice in my head saying, "Tart." I don't see why, though, because I am still a free woman. I haven't plighted my troth with Masimo. I haven't had a chance to plight anything, as he hasn't bothered to get in touch with me. I am officially an untrothed person.

Robbie suggested we go to La Strada, which is a cool Italian bar/coffeehouse sort of place with sofas and stuff. All the groovy types go there, it's perfect for showing off in.

three-quarters of an hour later

Robbie has been telling me about his time in Kiwi-a-gogo land. He's made me laugh quite a lot, but I must say there is a high level of tensionosity. He hasn't actually said anything that would make you think he was not just a mate, talking about wombats and sheep to another mate. He hasn't said,

"You're the one for me, Sex Kitty." Actually from my point of view it's a bit tricky thinking of safe things to talk about. I don't feel I can talk about the Stiff Dylans because then Masimo would come up (oo-er) and what would I say then? I don't know if anyone has snitched to Robbie about Masimo being my maybe boyfriend. I can tell you this for free, though, if anyone has said anything bitchy it will be Wet Lindsay. Using my world-famed subtletosity I must subtly find out, in a subtle way, what she has told him.

I said, "Erm, I heard that Wet . . . I mean Lindsay—turned up on the night you arrived back. Did she have any . . . er . . . news?"

He looked at me. "I didn't think you got on all that well with Lindsay."

I said, "Who does? I'm only human."

He laughed, thank goodness.

At which point, and this is unbelievable, Miss Octopushead herself walked into the bar with her indescribably dull and sad mates. She was flinging her hair about and doing that hippy walk thing which is vair vair common. (Unless I am doing it.) She went over to the bar and turned round to say something to ADM and that is when she saw us.

She looked like someone had just stuck a burning poker up her bum-oley. She turned back to the bar to order her drink and when she got it she walked over to our table. Oh brilliant, I was going to get a Coca-Cola over my head. But she ignored me completely and just spoke to Robbie. "Hi Robbie, great night on Saturday, I'll see you at the after-gig party next week. I'm looking forward to it."

Then she looked at me like she had just spotted a bit of gob having a cup of coffee and said, "Georgia, out a bit late, aren't you? Looking forward to going off camping with your little mates? It sounds ever so exciting and you will probably get to stay up late playing games and so on. I remember I used to love camping when I was your age. See you."

And she slimed off.

Oh I hate her.

Robbie looked at me. "She doesn't seem to really like you that much. Er, camping?"

I said, "We are being made to go and thrash around in the undergrowth for German. I should have never mentioned the Kochs."

Oh well done, brain, talking complete gibberish and mentioning the Kochs. Super. Thanks a lot. Good night.

Lindsay was talking in a really mad way to ADM, shaking her extensions and looking over at us. I was definitely a dead person when I got to Stalag 14. Lindsay was going to make it her life's work to kill me. At the very least I was going to be Stumpy the girl from Stump land.

As my brain was prattling merrily along by itself, Robbie looked over my shoulder toward the door. He said, "This is a popular place."

I looked round. Oh excellent, just when you think things can't get any worse, they get worserer. There at the door was Masimo with Dom from the Stiff Dylans. This was awful. Robbie and Masimo looked at each other and did that nodding thing that boys do. Masimo looked at me in a sort of odd way. I couldn't tell what he was thinking. Phwoar, I could tell what I was thinking, though, he is, it has to be said, gorgey porgey plus nine. And that is, as any fool can tell you, a lot of gorgey porgey.

He and Dom came over to our table and did a lot more of that boy stuff:

"How's it going, mate?"

"Cool."

"Are you cool?"

"Yeah, I'm cool. How are you?"

87

"Cool."

Total WUBBISH. I don't know why girls get told off so much for being superficial and only caring about makeup. Boys are worse, they never say anything that lets you know what is going on. Even if they have the fight to end all fights with someone and their head gets pulled off they'll say (with difficulty, because of the missing head-scenario), "No, it's fine, all cool. We're cool with it."

Masimo said to me, "*Ciao*, Georgia, how are you?"

I said, "Oh, me well I'm alrighty, as alrighty as . . . er . . . anything."

Shutup shutup shutup now.

The lads chatted for a bit about the band whilst I sat there like the goosegog fiasco of the year. Dom said, "Do you fancy coming and jamming with us at the gig?"

Then they started the cool thing again! Robbie said, "Yeah, that would be great if it's all cool with Masimo."

Masimo said, "For me, it would be OK, this would be a cool thing, per me, and you come and sing maybe a few of your songs. Yes?"

He was talking to Robbie, but looking at me. I

was just sitting there like a fool in a skirt (which I was). I could not think of anything except the last words I had said to Masimo, before I had run off for my imaginary train, which were, as I recall, "Did you see the footie scores this arvie?"

Perfect. What could be more sane than that?

"Anything" is the answer you are looking for.

Through the mists of horror and ordure, I heard Dom saying, "See you then, mate. Bye, Georgia."

And they all went off to another table. As they sat down, some girls from St. Mary's Sixth-form College came skittering in and joined them at their table. Doing that ridiculous kissing on both cheeks thing. Why were they sitting with them? One of the girls was whispering in Masimo's ear and flicking her hair about. What was going on?

Robbie said, "Shall we quit the scene? Do you fancy a bit of a stroll?" I managed to nod without my head falling off and we left the cafe. Lindsay looked absolute daggers at me as I went past her. I don't know what Masimo did as we left, I couldn't bear to look at him. I have never been so full of confusiosity in my life and that is truly saying something.

Robbie was a bit quiet as we walked along. He

had his hands in his pockets so at least I didn't have the lurking-arms scenario to worry about. As we got to North Street he stopped and turned to face me.

"Georgia, I know that when I left you were really upset and I am sorry that I hurt you so much. I just felt that you were so much younger than me and that . . ."

He stopped and looked into the distance.

What what? And that what? *And that I was wrong, you are so full of maturiosity, Georgia, that I would like to snog you within an inch of your life?* Is that what?

And that's when I felt a sort of dithery strange energy. Like there was a mad person behind me. There was.

"Oh, er, hiiiiiiiiiiiiiiiiiii . . . I was just out in the street, like I am now and I, well . . . Hi, Gee . . . hi, Robbie . . ."

Ellen. What was she doing? Lurking about like Lurkio in the streets. On her own. But not in casual gear. She was all tarted up. Was she following us? Hoping for a threesome? How weird and French. But no, she wasn't following us, because that is when I saw Dave the Laugh with his posse. Oh nooooooooo. I must hide, hide. I wish I could turn my skin to bark like those iguana things and then I could just blend in with the trees . . . What was I talking about? There were no trees, there were just shops, well I wish I could have skin like a shop then . . . and then . . . SHUT UP!!! Dave clocked us and came swanning up all full of casualosity and *joie de* whatsit and winked at me.

"Oy Robbie, Georgia . . . and oooh it's Ellen. What are you hep cats up to then?"

Ellen went absolutely purple, and was just opening and closing her mouth like a purple trout. She managed to say, "Oh Dave . . . wow . . . er . . . hi, fancy, fancy seeing you here . . . er . . . here . . . in with your . . .

Dave said, "Trousers on?"

Ellen went on and on, "Er no, no, not the trousers . . . well yes, because well you have got them on but . . . but . . . well anyway I must be going."

And she went off.

She must have been secretly trailing Dave

around. Blimey. I have eventually met someone who is even more full of bonkerosity than me.

Dave shouted after her, "Missing you already, Ellen."

That's done it, now we will spend the next month discussing with Ellen whether he, like, really was missing her already, and when was already and what did he mean by missing. I felt sorry for Ellen in an irritated way, because she really did luuurve Dave the Laugh. She has never forgotten the eight-and-a-half minutes they went out together.

Dave was looking very cool indeed, there is something about him that reeks of naughtinosity. And my lips started that puckering-up business all by themselves. And I did a bit of ad hoc hair swishing.

I'd missed seeing him.

He seemed completely at ease with me and Robbie. Didn't he mind that we might be going out together? He seemed to have forgotten about his "What if you really liked someone and then you lost them" fandango. Which is of course a good thing. Really good. I'm glad. That means we can just be mates. Which I like. As everyone knows.

Mateyness is my besty thing.

He said to me, "Nice skirt, Georgia. Has your grandad's girlfriend knitted you anything unusual lately? I saw her on the back of your grandad's bike the other day in a sort of one-piece thing, it may have been a knitted swimsuit. She's a goer, isn't she?"

I said, "That is one way of putting it."

Robbie said, "I didn't know your grandad had got a girlfriend. The last thing I heard from Tom was that he was arrested for being drunk in charge of a bike."

The boys laughed together. No, no, no, stop laughing about my stupid grandad, this was not the way things were supposed to be between love rivals.

two minutes later

When we reached the Buddha Lounge, Dave's posse said, "S'laters," and went off inside.

Dave said, "We're having a needle pool match, Robbie, if you fancy it. Or are you otherwise engaged?"

I went completely red and had to pretend to look for something in my bag.

Robbie said, "Maybe catch you later."

the gate to bonkers hall (i.e., my house)
10:00 p.m.

When we got to my gate Robbie looked me straight in the eyes. Oh goddy god he was going to snog me. He took his hands out of his pockets and I did my famous looking down and then looking up thing. At which point Mr. and Mrs. Next Door came along walking the Prat brothers. What is it with this town? Did someone on the radio say "Snogging alert, snogging alert. There is the chance that Georgia might actually have a snogathon with one of her many maybe boyfriends. Why not go out and annoy her by popping up unexpectedly?"

Mr. Next Door went all puffed up and insane when he saw me. He said, "Just the person I wanted to see."

Mrs. Next Door was saying, "Don't upset yourself, dear."

"Upset myself, upset myself!!! Do you know what that furry ruffian you call a pet has done now, do you? Do you?"

Actually I did have a bit of a clue, but I didn't say.

Mr. Next Door was going on and on.

"He has absolutely DECIMATED our aquarium. DECIMATED it. There were tadpoles all over the rockery. It's a bloody disgrace. In fact I have got a good mind to get onto the authorities and get it removed to a place where it won't be a danger to the public anymore."

I said, "Yes, I agree aquariums can be very dangerous."

I really thought that he was going to implode, so I said soothingly, "He's just high-spirited. He thinks the tadpoles are egging him on, waggling about like that. It's his nature, he's a hunter, he likes killing things."

Mr. Next Door said, "You don't have to tell me that."

Eventually he went off grumbling and moaning on and on, the Prat brothers yapping away. They had completely spoiled the snogging mood. Robbie said, "I'm going to get off now, Georgia, nice to see you."

He looked like he was going to say something else and then he just went, "See you at the gig."

And that was it. He did give me a little peck on the cheek, but what did that mean?

two minutes later
I watched him walk off down the street. He walked in a really cool way. I watched him right down to

the end of the street and he didn't even look back when he went around the corner.

10:15 p.m.
I have accidentally gotten home at a decent time. When I came in, Mutti just looked at me in amazement. She said, "You're in."

Then she went to the kitchen and came back with a bowl of cornflakes, which she gave me. I said, "Blimey, you never usually cook, Mum."

five minutes later
In bed lying down, just thinking.

one minute later
How weird is this?

five minutes later
So this is my wonderful life. I start off not knowing what going for coffee means and now I'm wondering what "see you at the gig" means. Does it mean see you at the gig, my new girlfriend, or see you at the gig, my old mate?

I may or may not have two boyfriends and none of us seem to know. And even if I did have two, maybe I only have one now because Masimo will think that I am going out with Robbie. But I'm not. Am I?

Goodie, now I am queuing up at the Bakery of Love, strapped to the rack of love, which makes it very difficult to even get inside the door in the first place.

Just then I heard baldy types sniggering in the hall outside my door.

Oh dear God, now what? Dad and Uncle Eddie have obviously been at the jungle juice because Uncle Eddie said in a really crap Chinese accent, "Special deliverly."

And underneath the door came a sort of postcard thing. I heard a piggy-type snort, from Vati.

It's unbelievable at their age. I suppose I will have to look, otherwise they will be crouching outside my door all night.

one minute later
Oh how vair vair amusant. The postcard said:

TEENAGERS, FED UP WITH BEING HARASSED
BY YOUR STUPID PARENTS? TAKE ACTION,
LEAVE HOME, GET A JOB, PAY YOUR OWN BILLS.
WHILST YOU STILL KNOW EVERYTHING.

I said, "Yeah, good one. Good night, you pranksters."

They went snorting off. Good grief.

two minutes later

Where was I? Oh yes, strapped to the rack of love, not being able to get through into the bakery. Well, how about if I undo the straps, chuck the rack away and enter boldly, shouting, "Give me a dozen mixed cakes, please!"

No, no, no, no, no! No to red bottomosity!!!

one minute later

What if I said, "Yes, I have made my selection. I would like the Italian cakey, please."

one minute later

No, no, no, make that the creamy Robbie éclair.

one minute later

On second thought, could I have the . . . Oh *sacré* bloody *bleu*, I will be up all night worrying about . . .

Zzzzzzzzzzz.

return of the hornmeister, quickly followed by the luurve god

wednesday july 20th

stalag 14

I have decided to gird my loins and take the high road, etc., or whatever it is that our Och Aye friends drone on about. Anyway I am going to be positive. And actually the day did start in tip-top form. First of all, Angus set fire to his own tail sitting near the oven. Which I have to say was very funny. Libby laughed so much I thought I would have to do the Heimlich maneuver on her. Which I think is an omen for everything going my way boywise.

Ran up to Jas at her gate and gave her a firm handshake and said, "This is the first day of the rest of our lives."

She said, "What does that mean?"

I said, "I don't know, but let's disco dance."

And we burst into a quick bout of the Viking

disco inferno dance. Well, the stabbing and leg-kicking. Jas wouldn't do the all-over body shake because she didn't want to mess up her fringe.

I told her a bit about my night, but I let there be an air of mysteriosity about things. Mostly I lied.

assembly

Slim was moaning on as usual. "Why is it necessary for me to remind you that the science block skeleton is not a toy? Whoever thought it was funny to dress it up in Mr. Attwood's spare overalls and sit it in his hut with a flask is very childish. Mr. Attwood got quite a start." Etc., etc., blah, blah, rave on, rave on. But then the music started (or Miss Wilson playing the crap piano, as some people call it), and we realized it was the *pièce de résistance* comedy hymnwise. Not Jerusalem. Obviously it would have been top if it had been Jerusalem with its famous refrain "And was Jerusalem builded here amongst England's dark satanic PANTS," but it was even better than that. Because yesssssss it was "Gladly my cross I bear." Or as we know and love it, "Gladly my cross-eyed bear." Oh yes. Klingon salutes all round for the ace gang.

Hawkeye was giving us the hairy eyeball

because normally we do not bother singing, we just mouth the words. But *touché*, Hawkeye, girl torturer and center of poonosity, today the ace gang has triumphed comedywise.

Then to put the icing on the pajamas, as we trooped out along the corridor, Elvis Attwood tripped over his mop and had a magnificent spaz attack and started hitting the mop. I think he is tipping over the edge into insanity and mentaldom.

blodge

Miss Finnigan is absent, probably exhausted by hauling her nungas around all day, they are quite literally giganticibus. Nearly as obscene as my mum's. As a special treat, Miss Wilson has been sent on as sub. Joy unbounded.

As we lolled into our seats, Miss Wilson was fiddling around with a TV. Rosie said, "Ooh good, is it *Gladiator*, Miss?"

Miss Wilson had a complete ditherama and practically lassoed herself with the electrical cable. She was all flushed.

"No, no, it's not *Gladiator* because it's—"

Rosie hadn't finished. "We are always allowed to watch *Gladiator* on Wednesdays. And as it is set in olden times we are also allowed to practice our Viking bison horn dance. Do you want to see it?"

Smoothing her bob in between plugging stuff in, Miss Wilson said, "Now Rosie, you know that it's biology and so I will be showing a relevant film. So settle down girls and . . . Julia, please do not set fire to the plants with the Bunsen burner; that is not what they are for."

Jools started then: "What are Bunsen burners for, then, Miss? I thought that was what the huge flame thing was for."

I didn't give Miss Wilson much chance of making it through to the end of the lesson.

five minutes later
Miss Wilson is sensationally red. Rosie offered to help plug stuff in and accidentally turned the fan full on, which nearly blew Miss Wilson's bob off. She has outdone herself fashionwise today. And I am not saying that just to be nice. She must have found the only corduroy shop in the world and today she was wearing a pinafore dress made out of it, with ankle socks. They were not made out of corduroy actually, but it would have been good if they had been.

I said to Mabs, "If this so-called film is anything to do with reproduction by any creature on the planet, I am definitely putting chewed-up paper in my earlugs."

two minutes later
The film turns out to be about bees. It is a film about a bee center.

How crap is this going to be?

an hour later
That was the best thing I have seen for ages. We made Miss Wilson rewind the bit where the two queens were having a bitch fight. I didn't know how fab bees were, and so sensible they could teach us a thing or two. For instance, the queen bee kills her sexual partners by tearing off their reproductive equipment (or bee trouser-snake addenda) once she has had her wicked way with them.

As I said to Jas, "That would solve my multi-boyfriend *problemo.*"

She said, "Georgia, excuse me if I am right, but one of your so-called boyfriends took you out for a coffee and didn't snog you, and the other one hasn't even got on the blower. That is not what I would call a multi-boyfriend *problemo*."

I kicked her shin.

"I hate you, Jas."

"Well I am only telling you the truth, that is what friends are for."

"Is it? Well I don't tell you how stupid your fringe looks, do I?"

"Yes."

She is so unreasonable and mad. And so full of herself just because she has a boring old boyfriend. However, for once I don't mind because I feel that I have learned quite a lot today. I may become a beekeeper/model/backing singer.

Did you know that baby bees are fed bee bread? That is *le* fact.

Also, when they sting you they lose their bottoms.

on the way to english

Miss Wilson is beside herself at the prospect of going camping. As we left blodge she said, "Girls, it's going to be such fun."

I said to the gang, "I tell you this for free, I am not doing anything to do with mime or clowning, and that is final."

english

Blimey O'Reilly, how many plays did Billy Shakespeare write? He can't have got out much. Apparently most of the rude words we know are from him and his mates, so I don't know why we get told off for using them. And also, violence and binge-drinking is not exactly a new invention. Billy and his fellow twits in tights were not exactly kind to each other. For a laugh they used to put people in stocks and so on. In fact that was their entertainment, that and baiting bears. For instance, here is a real conversation between Elizabethan mates, Tight-us Tight-us and Mind-us My cod-us Piece.

Mind-us My Cod-us Piece: "Prithee Tight-us Tight-us, what do you fancy doing tonight-us?"

T. T.: "Sirre what-us about drinking a pint or two of gin and annoying-us the bears?"

M.C.P.: "Nah . . . Let-us just bugger off down to the stocks and throw tomatoes at the weirdo."

french

I am going to have to kill Rosie because unfortunately she has got prepreweekend bonkerosity. Or a touch of the Svens, as some might say. She has just sent me a French joke.

Her notelet said: *"Bonjour, mon petit pain.*
What do you call a French man in sandals?
Au revoir.
Rozeeeeeeeeeeee"
I wrote back, "I don't care."
But she gave me her raised eyebrows and nodding head thing until I had to mouth to her, "Oh go on then."
And she wrote back, "Philippe Philoppe."

on the way home
4:15 p.m.
The Blunderboys are trailing along behind us doing what they think is gay repartee. Saying things, like, "Hey love, lie down, will you? I need somewhere to park my bike."

What are they talking about? I'll tell you this, they will be the last to know.

After about ten minutes of this I turned round to them and said, "Er, why don't you go away. A LOT?"

And amazingly that baffled them. I think it was having a clear instruction that they couldn't cope with. Apparently boys and dogs have stuff in common. That is what the Hornmeister told me once.

At that moment, as if he had been earwigging in my brain, the Hornmeister appeared over the horizon with two of his mates. When he saw us he did this mad running toward us with his arms outstretched. Sort of skipping like from *The Sound of Music*.

"Hello ladeeeeeeez, the vati is back! Sound out the pants of England!!! Let the Cosmic and General Horn be heard! Hooooorrnnnnnnn!!! Who are my bitches???"

Ellen said, "Er, we are . . . er are we your, erm, bitches?"

We looked at her.

I said in a dignified at all times way, "Oh hello Dave, you're not going to do your rapping thing and then fall over a wall again, are you?"

He looked at me and licked his lips. Honestly.

"Georgia, I know that is just your little way of saying, 'Hey big boy, hold me back because you give me the Horn big time.'"

I just looked at him. I wasn't going to smile at him, if that is what he thought. He was too full of himself and his red bottomosity. But he would not get me to . . . oh blimey, I have accidentally given him my full nostril–flaring smile! Damn. He linked up with us all and then his two mates did the same so that we looked like we were doing the hokey-pokey. I hope we didn't have to negotiate any lamp-posts or the elderly insane.

He said, "Trot on, girls. Do you like my new trainers? I feel like Jack the Biscuit in them."

They were quite cool, as it happens.

One of his mates, Declan, was linked up to Ellen, and he said, "We had a laugh today, there was a minor rumble in the corridor because Phil the Nerd and his mates tried to be top dog in the lunch queue. So clearly he had to be binned. Excellent."

I knew I shouldn't ask, but somehow I did. "What do you mean he had to be binned?"

in my bedroom

I know that I have said this many, many times, but boys are a bloody mystery. Apparently when they get bored, boys go on a "binning" session. They got Phil the Nerd and put him botty-first into a litter bin. As soon as he managed to heave himself out, his "mates" put him back in. Then when he got out again, Dave and Dec and company turned up and put him back in again. And so on until the end of break. Why?

5:30 p.m.

I hate to admit this because of my position as mate to Dave the Laugh, but there is something that goes on in the jelloid knicker department when I see him. He's sort of familiar somehow, and he does make me laugh. But shut up, brain, because mates do not snog or even think about snogging. That is *le* fact. I have too many maybe boyfriends to worry about without thinking about Dave the Laugh and his snogging abilities. Which I'm not even thinking about, by the way.

two minutes later

I was just thinking about when I first snogged him at the Fish party. That really was the beginning of my red-bottom phase. I blame him. He started me on the slippery slope with his lip-nibbling techniques and so on. But I will just LET IT GO because he is not on the snoggees list, he is just a boymatetypefandango. Which is good.

one minute later

I wonder what number he has got up to with his "girlfriend." He never mentions her. Mind you, *I* never mention her.

I wonder if she mentions herself.

I wonder if she has ever asked him about me.

She isn't with him much; perhaps he has dumped her.

ten minutes later
A lot of thumping on the stairs.

"Come on dollyboy, Josh boy, bring pussycat in here lalalalalalalala. Pussycat pussycat where have you beeeeeen, I've been to London to see a sardine!!! Hahahahahahaha."

My door crashed open and a very red-faced sister loomed round. She had Gordon by the neck and he was struggling like billio. Yeah, good luck, furry chum. She had her other chubby little arm around the neck of her "boyfwend" the unfortunate Josh. Libby lobes Josh. She treats him just like the rest of her toys (Pantalitzer doll, Angus and Gordy, Scuba-diving Barbie, Jesus, Sandra, me), really really badly. The only difference is that as yet she hasn't been able to remove bits of his body. Pantalitzer doll is quite literally just a head now.

"Heggo Gingie, my Gingie, I LOBE my Gingie. Kiss Joshie the dollyboy."

"No, Libbs, I don't think that Josh wants a kiss,

and you are holding him too tightly round his little neck his head is going red, isn't it, Joshie?"

Libby smiled her alarming smile. Lately she has taken to opening her eyes really wide when she does it and sticking her teeth out, like a bonkers hamster who has just seen a really big carrot.

"He laaaikes it."

And she dragged them off into her room. If I hear sawing noises, I will go in. Although why I have to take responsibility I don't know. What are my "parents" doing? If they aren't interested in their children, they shouldn't have them. I might say that to them. I might say . . . no hang on a minute I know what will happen then, they WILL start taking an interest in me, just to annoy me.

Went down to run myself a bath and as I passed Libby's door I could hear her talking.

"Now then, a bitty lit of lipstick. Mmmmmm."

Josh is going to look like a toddler drag queen by the time his mum picks him up. Still, if she bans him from coming round it might save him from something far, far worse.

As I came out of the bathroom, Vati was coming out of the kitchen. Wearing what he likes to think as "leisure wear." Essentially jeans and a

T-shirt that says, "I'm a grown up. So nananananananana."

How pathetico. But I didn't say anything. He started rambling and moaning, though. He only has to see my head to start complaining.

"Georgia, you had better not be in that bathroom for the rest of the night, there are other people in this house, you know."

I said, "I know, that is what I complain about as well."

"Don't be so bloody cheeky. The day you start paying the water bill is the day you can start being cheeky."

Oh drone on. Just because as yet I am not the girlfriend of a popstar and a squillionnaire beekeeper backing singer etc., I am picked on by old huge botty. Still, live and let die, is what I say.

If Mum and Dad were bees, he would be a dead bee by now. And that is not easy to say.

He hadn't finished, though. "And feed your bloody cat, it's attacking my trousers."

Who wouldn't, I thought, but I didn't say that.

I turned the bath on and went into the kitchen. When he saw me, Angus shot through the cat flap into the garden. Then he came back in doing his comedy coming through the cat flap backward thing and yowling like he hadn't eaten anything for days. I know that is not true because of the complaints from the neighbors. Mr. Up the Road said that Angus even ate some lard he had put out for the birds. The Prat brothers have to be fed inside now because Angus is so sneaky he can dart out within seconds and gobble down their food. He is like the James Bond of Cat Land—they seek him here, they seek him there, they seek that puddy tat everywhere. I have seen him leap down from the bedroom windowsill unexpectedly, right into the Prat poodles' food bowl. Or the roof. Or out of the dustbin. You have to admire him, really.

Owwwwwwwww. Bloody hell, I think he may have eaten my ankle.

I put Angus's food in his bowl and he was purring and pushing himself against my legs. Aahhh. Then he sat on the table and just looked.

I said, "Don't you want your kitty-cat food?"

He shut his eyes.

I went and checked the bath and put in some of Mum's strictly banned expensive bath oil that she hides in her wardrobe. Honestly, it is so tiring trying to have a bath around this place.

When I went back into the kitchen, Angus was sitting in his food in the food bowl.

I don't know what to say.

As I was just looking at him and he was looking at me, Gordy came into the kitchen. Fully made up. Honestly. If I didn't know better I would say that he had false eyelashes on. He was covered in foundation and rouge, and around his eyes were big black rings and some sort of blue stuff. I noticed he had some clip-on earrings on as well. And a bow on his tail.

I went off into the bathroom.

The odd thing was, Gordy looked strangely happy.

Maybe he is a homosexualist cat.

Angus will disown him.

in the bathroom

Aah, at last I can relax and think about myself properly.

It is amazing how floaty nungas are. I wonder why. Perhaps it is in case of flooding and then girls, who of course are the most important sex, would float to safety.

It may be a genetic floaty survival thingy.

two minutes later

I don't like to criticize Big G unnecessarily, but it does on the whole seem like a useless genetic floaty survival thingy. Much the same as the body-hair fiasco. What is the point of having rogue hairs shooting out of the back of your knee, for instance? Or the big curly one I found in my eyebrow? How could that help the human race survive? Unless there was a time when wild animals were really really frightened of eyebrows.

Back to the nungas, though. (I can hear Dave the Laugh saying, "Yes, let us get back to the nungas, Kittykat!" Shutup shutup, Dave the Laugh's imaginary voice! Get out of my bath!!!!) Where was I? Oh yes, if it is down to floatiness, clearly Wet Lindsay would sink without a trace, as she has got pretendy nungas, which is a GOOD thing, but Melanie Griffiths would be floating around with me for sure. I mean she's alright and everything, but not exactly tip-top brainwise. I wouldn't want her and me to be responsible for repopulating the earth after a flood.

fifteen minutes later

I heard the doorbell ring. Please let it not be

Grandad in his bicycling shorts, with Maisie his knitted girlfriend. Thank goodness I have the door safely bolted. I could hear muffled voices as I put my face mask on. Aaahh this was the first time I had been relaxed for ages, well since I had my little zizz in maths this arvie. I find trigonometry vair vair soothing.

two minutes later
Dad said through the door, "Georgia, are you still in the bath?"

Uuuurgh, my dad was talking to me whilst I was in the nuddy-pants! How disgusting. I put a flannel over my nungas.

"Dad, go away."

"There is someone to see you."

What? The ace gang usually rings before they come round. I bet it was Mr. Next Door come to complain about his stupid aquarium fiasco, but I hadn't heard any shouting.

I said, "Who is it?"

Then I heard his voice. "Georgia . . . *ciao*, it is Masimo. I came for to see you. How are you?"

I couldn't believe it, I couldn't believe that I was talking to Masimo in the nuddy-pants. Me, not him, I mean, unless it was an Italian tradition to call round at a girl's house with no clothes on. You never know, of course, but . . . shut up shut up!!!

This called for hidden depths of sophisticosity. Maybe I could pretend I wasn't in the bath, that I was just, like, in the bathroom. No, no, that was much worse because if I wasn't having a bath what was I doing in the bathroom? He might think there was a loo in here. There IS a loo in here. Oh no nononnooooooo. Why had my stupid stupid father let him come near the bathroom door???

I could hear my dad say, "I know she is in there because I spoke to her just before you came round. Who knows what girls do in there, eh? Where did you say you came from in Italy?"

Masimo said in his gorgey Pizza-a-gogo way, "It is a small place near Roma."

I stepped very, very quietly out of the bath. Don't make a ripply water noise, just shushhyshush. I needn't have bothered, though, because Dad was still pratting on for England.

"Oh yes, very nice, I went on a footie excursion with the lads to Rome, had a lot of your *vino tinto*!!! *Muchos* nice."

Masimo laughed.

"Ah yes, I like to play footie. When I go home I with my mates we play in a how you say, in a league."

"Yes, I like to keep in top condition myself. Would you like a drink?"

"Ah well, thank you, that would be nice, Mr. Nicolson."

"Call me Bob."

And I heard them go off into the kitchen.

Call me Bob???

No, I tell you what, why don't we call you "You big fat prat!!!"

How could this be happening? I could have drowned in the bath for all they knew.

I dried myself and washed off the face mask.

But I was still trapped in the bathroom with no makeup on, with a Luurve God just two inches of wood away. Oh what should I do? There was nothing to improvise with, makeupwise. Mum told me that Maisie used to use shoe polish as eyeliner because they were so poor in the olden days. And bite her lips to make them go red. Come to think of it, she looks like the bride of Dracula now, so years of lip biting have paid off. Grandad likes that living dead look.

I put my ear to the door and I could just make

out my dad pratting on and on about his football "career," i.e. being generally a large lazy lardy lump on legs. Then I heard Mum come out of the lounge and shout up the stairs, "Libby, you and Josh are very quiet. What are you doing?"

I heard a bit of scuffling and then Libby saying, "Nothing, Mummy."

And I thought I heard Josh shout, "Help!" but I had no time for toddler trouble just now. I had my own emergency.

I whispered as loudly as I could, "Mum! Mum!!!"

She came over to the door.

"What? Why are you still in there? Masimo is here. God, he's gorgeous, isn't he?"

"Mum, I am stuck in here in my crappy T-shirt and joggy bums and no makeup. What are you going to do about it? Because if you don't help me, I will be in here for the rest of my life."

She said, "Say please."

"PLEASE help me, Mum. Otherwise I will kill you."

Eventually after she had made me plead properly, Mum went off and sneaked me in my makeup bag and jeans.

My hand was all trembly and my face had that

attractive red quality that you long for when you have a Luuurve God in the house. Anyway, I did my best. I thought I would go for that "ooooh you caught me washing my hair" scenario. So mascara, eyeliner, lippy and lip gloss and a towel around my hair (to disguise the fact that my hair looked like an elephant had had a poo on it).

Big deep breath and open the door.

in the kitchen

Oh this is sooooo embarrassing. Vati is trying to talk to us like we are all mates. Why doesn't he just go away? Forever???

He had one leg up on a chair drinking his beer and saying to Masimo, "So have you got a motor, then, Mas?" (Mas . . . ohmygod he was calling him Mas!!!)

Masimo was looking at me, but he said, "Er, oh no, I have a scooter."

I said, "Do you want to, erm, go and sit outside for a bit? And chat?"

Mum came in, dragging Josh and Libby with her. My worst fears were realized—Josh was dressed as a drag queen. A drag queen with half a Mohican haircut.

Mum was livid.

"What is Josh's mummy going to say? You naughty girl, I told you not to play with scissors."

Libby was very cross as well.

"He's been to London to see the sardine."

Dad said, "Don't be cheeky, young lady."

Libby put her hands on her hips and shouted at him, "DON'T YOU be cheeky, bad mummy!!!"

As Dad was momentarily distracted by being called mummy, I said to Masimo, "Quickly, let's get out of here."

And we went and sat on the wall. I made sure we were hidden by the tree so that M and D couldn't spy on us from the house.

I still had my hair up in a towel, but I like to think it made me look a bit like a Thai bride or something. That is what I like to think.

At first we just sat there in silence, I didn't know what to do.

Eventually I said, "I'm sorry about the train fandango, Robbie turning up like that, and you saying you're free for me, and then I was carrying the horns . . . I just went a bit mad."

Masimo didn't say anything. Oh no. Then I felt his hand on my face and he turned my face toward him and looked me straight in the eye. I am melting, I am melting!!!

"Georgia, for me, it is the same. For you, I don't know, I see you with Robbie in the cafe and he is nice guy, you for him was liking before. So I don't know."

You and me both, pally. You for me don't know. But fortunately I didn't say that. I didn't know what to say. I was just looking in his eyes, his lovely yellow cat eyes, and then he kissed me on the mouth. Really gently. Then he did it again. And my naughty lips started going on snogging alert. He put his other hand on the back of my neck and pulled me nearer to him. I hope my towel doesn't fall off and reveal mad elephant poo hair. This time he kissed me long and hard. It was so groovy and warm and I couldn't tell where his mouth finished and mine started and then . . . some absolute arse shouted, "Oy, does his boyfriend know you are snogging him?"

We both looked up and couldn't see anyone, then I noticed a bit of a rustling behind the hedge of Mr. Across the Road's garden. I leapt across and looked over the hedge and there in his ridiculous sports cap was Oscar, otherwise known as junior Blunderboy and tosser.

I leapt over the hedge, gave him a swift kick in the kidneys and then hopped back to Masimo. Masimo was laughing.

"Georgia, everyone is here, it is how you say, very busy. . . ."

He smiled at me and got up and sat on his scooter.

I looked at him.

He looked at me.

He said, "So, Miss Georgia, now, what shall we do? I am free for you. Are you free for me also?"

Good point. Well made. But what was the answer?

I started thinking about mentioning my untrothness, but then thought about trying to describe that to anyone normal, and also Italian.

Instead I took a deep breath and said, "I really like you, and think you are the bee's knees, etc."

Masimo said, "I am the knees of a bee?"

I said, "Well, forget about the bee thing, it's just that . . . well, I think I have to talk to Robbie first properly."

Masimo smiled a little smile. "Yes, I think so, too. It is fair."

I watched him go down to the bottom of our road on his scooter. Oh no, now what had I done? I had practically refused to go out with a Luuurve God. I was clearly mentally deranged.

I watched him get to the end of our street and indicate left . . . and then he did a big u-y and came hurtling back, screeching to a halt in front of me.

He said, "Georgia, I forgot for what I came to tell you, I am going home to Italy after the gig for a month to see my family. Can you, would you, if you decide you are free for me, come and stay with me, with my family for a little?"

Wow. We were practically married!!! And me in my towel!!!

I didn't really know what to say, so he said, "Think about this, *caro*, it would be beautiful."

And he rode off.

I floated past King Buffoon (Dad), cleaning his car, and I didn't even laugh when he said, "Fancy giving me a hand polishing the old Lovemobile?"

in the kitchen

Mum has tried to make Josh look like a human being, but the hair is scary. His mother will definitely inform the authorities. But ho hum, pig's bum. I said as I went to my bedroom, "Don't bother booking me up to go to Ireland with you, Mum as I will be holidaying just near Rome this summer."

She didn't even bother to reply, which is a bit rude, but typical of her self-obsessed attitude.

thursday july 21st
8:30 a.m.

Walking to Stalag 14 with Jas. I told her about Masimo coming round and snogging me. She said, "So what number did you get to?"

"Well, I suppose officially it was only a number four, but his mental vibe was more like eight."

"Are you saying that mentally he was doing upper-body fondling indoors?"

"Yep, I certainly am."

"But you were sitting on your wall outside."

"Well, officially but . . ."

"And he had his hand on the back of your neck, which is not your upper body."

"Yes it is."

Jas was chewing on her chuddie and had that annoying look on her face like she was thinking. I hate that. She was droning on and on like Mrs. Droning on Knickers, which she is.

"OK, in that case, if upper-body fondling doesn't mean your nungas, it just means anything on the top of your waist. Then number seven and eight could be like nose fondling or chin fondling."

God, she is soooooo annoying. And fringey.

"Jas, I am just trying to tell you what happened, this is not the Spanish Inquisition. You are not El Quasimodo."

She got into her Huffmobile then. "I didn't make these snogging rules up, Georgia, you did."

We were just passing a litter bin and for a minute of ecstasy I thought about shoving her in botty-first like Dave and his mates did. But actually if I did shove her in there, she might get stuck because of her enormous pantaloonies and I would have to call the fire brigade to cut her out. Besides which, I must remember I want to stay at her house on Saturday night after the gig in case there are any ad-hoc snogging opportunities—so there's no chance of Vati picking me up in his circus clown car.

So instead of hitting her or anything, I just smiled my loveliest smile and said, "Jas, you know that you are my besty pal, and like the Wise Woman of the Forest to me. Can I just tell you what happened?"

She flicked her fringe about and said,
then."

I told her all about the Italian holiday
Even she was quite impressed by that.

"Wow, well that is like almost being an official
girlfriend, isn't it? You are really going to have to
decide soon. But you don't really know if Robbie
likes you, do you? I mean you know he likes you like
matewise, but does he think you are girlfriend
material? I couldn't stand being you, not knowing
who my boyfriend was and everything. I was with
Tom last night and we were just, you know, rear-
ranging my owl collection into sizes together . . . it
was really, oh I don't know, and then he got hold of
my hand and put my fingers in his mouth and
sucked them."

I said, "Blimey, hand snogging, what number is
that on the scale?"

Jas said, "I dunno, four and a half, do you
think? It was only the fingers not the whole hand."

I didn't ask her who she knew that could fit a
whole hand in their mouth because it was all
making me feel a bit queasy.

stalag 14

9:30 a.m.

Wet Lindsay is on my case big time. As I was passing her to go to games, she said, "Walk properly."

What does that mean?

tennis courts

I was playing singles against Melanie Griffiths. Honestly, it shouldn't really be allowed. Her nungas are definitely a health hazard. I don't think she can really see over them to hit the ball. I was winning, by about eight-five-million–nil. The most dangerous times were when she had to bend over to pick up the balls. Quite often I thought she was just going to topple over.

Then Wet Lindsay and Astonishingly Dim Monica came sliming along and actually came into the court and sat down on the chairs by the net. Wet Lindsay was just looking at me, and if looks could kill, I would be deader than a dead person on dead tablets. In dead land.

She looked at me but went on talking to ADM really loudly. "If I had a big nose I think I would find it very difficult to disguise. It is just something you really can't get away from, isn't it? I mean, people say Barbra Streisand is a good singer, but mostly they say, "What an enormous nose."

I didn't mean to, but I found myself sucking in my nostrils as I was serving. Maybe I could just accidentally serve and knock her off her chair. I didn't dare, though, because she would probably snitch to Miss Wilson or Hawkeye and I would be made to polish Mr. Attwood's spade collection for the rest of my life.

Octopushead hadn't finished, though.

"I don't know what to do about Masimo and Robbie, I mean they are both gorgeous. Aren't they? And you don't want to upset anyone's feelings, but . . ."

I could see as I was dashing around the court, and waiting for Melanie to regain her balance, that ADM was nodding away like a nodding dog-person. Lindsay was rambling on, flicking her stupid extensions and crossing her nobbly knees. God, I hate her. On and on she went.

"I feel in a way, though, that Robbie has sort of blown it with me, he went away and so on when we had been quite serious. So if his work comes first, you would never be really sure that he was totally there for you. But he is so keen, you know? And of course Masimo has that Latin charm, and . . ." She raised her voice.

"Absolutely fantastic in the snogging area. I mean they do know how to do it, don't they, the Italians."

The bell rang just as Melanie actually really did reach down for the ball and fall over forward into the net. I went to help her get to her feet and as Wet Lindsay and ADM left the court, Lindsay said, "Your backhand is pretty weak, Nicolson, maybe when you grow up a bit you can take on proper players."

She seems like she is talking about tennis, but I know very well what she is talking about.

ace gang headquarters
lunchtime

I am absolutely livid about Lindsay and what she said. Is any of it true? Is she really snogging Masimo when I am practically his child bride?

I told the ace gang all the news.

Ro Ro said, "So Masimo came round and snogged you and asked you to go to Pizza-a-gogo land, but you think that he might be double-timing you with Wet Lindsay?"

Jools said, "Who do you like best—Robbie or Masimo?

I said, "I don't know what to think."

Ro Ro said, "This is when you need your mates around you to give you the benefit of their wisdom-osity. Hand me my beard."

We all sat around and watched her as she put on her beard and then launched herself into a solo version of the Viking disco inferno dance. It was, even if you live in Confusiosity House, Confusion Lane, East Confusion (which I did), vair vair *amusant*.

Then she sat down again, panting, and said, "If only I had a pipe, but Sven took it to college with him today. He wanted to repaint it for Saturday. Did I tell you that he has got a job djing now?"

Dear God.

Then she said, "What we must remember is that boys are quite literally a mystery, and as it says in the book, we have to keep them on the elastic band. Let them go wild and free and then they will come pinging back. I know that Sven comes pinging back with a vengeance. I have the love bites to prove it."

Jools said, "This is the plan: We have to be on high alert on Saturday at the Dylans gig and see what we think. You know, see if Masimo gives any signals that he likes Lindsay or if Robbie likes you as a girlfriend-type person."

Jas said, "Why would he do that? He's not mad."

I gave her my worst look. But actually the whole thing is giving me the mega droop. I said, "Even I don't know which one I really like. I mean, I did like the Sex God first. He was the one I first snogged."

Jas, or Mental the Memory Man, as she should be known said, "Well that is not true, is it? Because you snogged whelk boy first and then you let Mark Big Gob snog you and put his hand on your basoomas, almost on the first date. Which makes you a bit of a slag, actually. Perhaps Masimo has heard your reputation. A woman has to be very careful about her honor."

Right, that was it, I was going to turn her big fat knickers inside out and ram her into a sports locker at the very first opportunity I had.

Rosie said, "What has been happening snogwise to everyone? Anything to report? I have. I'll just say this . . . hello, number eight."

The result of the snogging survey is that Ro Ro and Sven are in the lead with an eight. Upper-body fondling indoors. Ellen lags behind on four "or something, I mean, is it, well I don't know if I . . ." Most of the others are on five. Jas, after a lot of red-faced looning about, admitted that she and Nature Boy had also "sort of" got to No. 7. I said that officially I was on 7, but mentally I thought really it was 8. Jas meanly said, "You mean you are on virtual eight."

I gave her my worst look, but she pretended she was sunbathing. After a bit I said to Jools, "So Jools, where are you at with Rollo?"

Jools astonished us all by saying that she had got to No. 9.

I went, "What, bwa? Below-waist activity???"

She said, "Well sort of."

"Sort of???"

We were all looking at her. This was amazing.

It turned out that she had shown Rollo her panties as a dare in the street.

I said, "Is that it?"

And she said, "Well, I shook my hips about a bit. He seemed to like it."

I don't know if I can stand much more of this. I may have to go and be a lesbian beekeeper.

in bed

I have got my hair in rollers for extra bounceability. I bet boys don't go through this. I can't imagine a bloke lying in bed with big prickly things in his head.

two minutes later

I know boys do stuff that they think will make them more attractive to girlies, like having a long fringe and so on. Walking along with their hips thrust forward and their hands in their pockets. Wearing pongey stuff that some fool in advertising says is irresistible to women, and that as soon as they smell it they want to get to No. 6 with you.

I passed Oscar the trainee tosser this evening and practically passed out. I have NEVER smelled stronger Brut or Impulse or whatever it is. I was choking. I tell you what, if he lights up a fag as well, that will be the end of him.

one minute later

I could offer him a fag and retreat to a safe distance.

friday july 22nd

Got up at the crack of 8:00 a.m. Looked at myself in the mirror. Is that the beginning of a lurker on my chin? Nooooo. I quickly squirted the lurking lurker with my perfume. No boy alive likes a girl with two chins and that is *le* fact. Well, unless Slim has got a boyfriend, in which case there is someone on the planet who likes a woman who has eighteen or nineteen chins. And not all of them on her head. Hahahaahahahaha. Oh dear God, I have got pre-boyfriend-choosing hysteria.

8:20 a.m.

My charming but insane sister is on the telephone. The fact that she has the receiver upside down and that there is no one on the other end of it doesn't seem to spoil her little chat. She was saying, "I know, yes, yes, Mr. Bum Bum is coming to school today in his poo pants! Hehe-hehehahahahaha lalalalalala."

Then she started snorting and shouted, "Bye-bye arsey!!!" and slammed down the receiver. When she saw me she came over and wanted to be picked up. She's not small and quite hefty. I had to lean against the door to use it as a support.

Once I had managed to pick her up, she started kissing me.

"I lobe you, I lobe you, my hairy sister, I loooooooooobe you."

Hairy sister? Had she seen something I hadn't? Had the orangutan gene leaped out to be friends with the lurker? I put her down and distracted her by saying, "Look, Bibbs, Angus is doing a big poo in Vati's tie drawer."

Which actually he was. I went into the bathroom.

one minute later

No, all seemed in order rogue-hairwise. I was quite literally smoothy smooth as a baby's bottom but without the bulging nappy scenario.

my bedroom
6:00 p.m.

For once in my life I have already decided what to wear on Saturday. My new leather skirt, ankle boots and crossover top.

That's it. Thank goodness I have decided. I can just concentrate on makeup and hair now.

five minutes later

Ankle boots or my pink shoes?

two minutes later

I hate my leather skirt, it's really naff.

three minutes later

Blue dress, then. That's the one.

five minutes later

Do I really want to look like a chav?

6:30 p.m.

I went downstairs and outside to sit on the wall. It was still really warm. I could see Mr. and Mrs. Next Door out in their garden having what they fondly imagine is a Mediterranean supper, but I don't know many Italians who have egg on toast for din-dins. With chipolatas. Also they are glaring at me. Italians don't glare, they sing and caress their guitars. Still, if Mr. and Mrs. Next Door want to eat mini hot dogs and glare, that is their choice. They are having a nice time; that is what counts. My new philosophy is I am going to enjoy my life and just see what happens. As Jas says, when I let her,

"*Que sera sera*, whatever will be will be."

Because "I have no time for fussing and fighting, my friends," as some pop legends said once.

Because, and I think it was the same pop legends that said, "Love is all you need. Nanananananaaaaaaa."

Love is what really matters. Not what mad neighbors with massive arses eat for their supps. Or what clothes a girl who may or may not be loved by so many Luuurve Gods wears.

It's not the dress that counts, it's the heart pumping underneath the dress.

five minutes later
Phoned Jas.

"Jas, what shall I wear tomorrow?"

"What?"

"Tomorrow, for the gig of my life, what shall I wear?"

"I'll tell you what not to wear, don't wear any high heels in case you have to run off and catch a train like last time!" And then she started laughing and honking like an annoying goose. I could hear someone else laughing as well.

I said, "Jas, that is a really crap thing to say for

a besty sort of person, and who is that laughing in the background?"

"It's Tom, he's helping me pack for the camping trip."

I so wanted to hit her. But I had to stay calm because of wanting to stay at her place on Saturday night. What is more, I had to listen to her listing the really, really boring things that she is looking forward to doing when we are camping. Who could possibly be interested in building a nighttime "hide" that you can crouch in and watch ferrets and badgers and so on do all the inde- scribably boring stuff that they do at nighttime? Digging and pooing mostly. Well, Jas is riveted by that sort of tosh.

She said, "If we are really lucky, Tom says we might see some foxes."

I said, "Yippppeee," in a sarcastic way, but then I remembered staying over at her house and had to change it to a sort of "Yipppeeee, I do hope we do see some foxes and maybe even some, erm, goats."

Jas said, "Why would we see any goats, they are not wandering about in the woods, are they? They would be on farms."

I said, "Perhaps they are bored with farm life and fancy getting out a bit, making new woodland friends and so on."

"You are being silly now."

"Jas, I am just remarking that it doesn't seem fair that all the foxes and badgers and so on who do not as far as I know lift a paw to help others, should be allowed to wander willy-nilly in the woods and the poor old goats, who give milk and so on should have to stay in. That is all I am saying."

"I am going now."

And she put the phone down.

one minute later

She is soooo annoying, but I must remember that I need to stay at her place after the gig. I phoned her back.

"Jas?"

"What?"

"Please don't get upset about the goats."

"You were being silly."

"I know, but it's only because I'm all nervous and excited. Please be my pal. Pleasey please please?"

"Well . . ."

"I promise to be excited if we see some foxes."

After about ten minutes of nicenosity, Jas forgave me. Phew. Thank goodness. Having a best pally is the most v. important thing in the world. Your pals will be with you, even though Luuurve Gods may come and go.

Also, she has said I can stay at her place. Hurray!

in the kitchen
Mum was making some snacks. She said, "So tell me, what is happening tomorrow?"

Oh God. Still, I had better tell her something as it looks like I might have to borrow her Chanel bag again. Even though I am banned for life after spilling hot chocolate in it. I said, "Well, you remember there is a gig on and that I am going to stay over at Jas's because it is nearer."

"It's not nearer if Dad picks you up in the car."

"Yes, but that is not going to happen."

"Why, have you asked him?"

"No, it is not going to happen, because it is not going to happen."

"And besides that, I don't remember saying you could stay at Jas's."

"You said I could go to the gig last week."

"I know, but what has that to do with staying at Jas's?"

"I ALWAYS stay at Jas's after gigs."

"No you don't."

"Well if I don't it's only because you want to spoil my life."

"What?"

"You know how important tomorrow is. I told you about Robbie, and then Masimo came round when I was in the bath and so on, and I STILL am not allowed to dye my hair, so I look like a boring person, and I have to traipse along to the gig with my ordinary hair whilst EVERYONE else is allowed to dye their hair. And now you are telling me that even though you said I could stay at Jas's, now you don't even know about it. I give up. I tell you what, I will just stay in my room for the rest of my life. Are you HAPPY now?"

ten minutes later

Mum was so frazzled by me that she has let me stay at Jas's! Yessssss! And borrow her bag!!!

So even though I will be naked tomorrow because I can't decide what to wear, I will at least have a nice bag.

in bed snuggled down

If I go to sleep early, then time will pass quickly and it will be tomorrow, today if you see what I mean.

I do.

Night-night.

9:00 p.m.

I am going to make a pro and con list of all the good and bad qualities of the Sex God and the Luuurve God. Now let me see, I'll start with the most important things.

Looks.

twenty minutes later

This is it.

Masimo:

Looks: A ten deffo.

Special attributes: Cat's eyes, Pizza-a-gogo charisma.

Snogging skills: *Muchos buenos.*

Sense of humor: Probably. Hard to tell. I haven't heard any Italian-type jokes yet. Or maybe I have but just don't understand them.

Personality: Yes.

Caring: Yes, because when he was finishing

with his ex, he was quite nice and everything. Also, even though I didn't like it, he was straight with me when he said he would think about going out with me.

Minus points.
Hmmmmmm.
There might be a touch of the "oooohhh mind my hair, do you like my handbag?"about him.
Although thinking about it, I don't know that I have actually noticed the "handbag, mind my hair" business. But Dave the Laugh has mentioned it. A LOT.
But Junior Blunderboy did shout out, "Does his boyfriend know you are snogging him?" Does that mean that there is the suggestion of the homosexualist about him?
The Wet Lindsay factor. Does not seem to entirely realize what a complete arse above all arses she is. On the plus side, he has not spent more than one or two evenings in her company. As far as I know. Ergo, may not have snogged her. Even though she has implied that he has . . .

Now then, over to Robbie.

Looks: Yummy scrumboes. Maybe, though, just for scrupulous accuracy and fairness, I should mark him down half a point because I do prefer yellow eyes to blue ones. So let's say nine and a half.

Special attributes: Ability to get on with me even when my brain has slipped off for a little holiday. Is nice about Angus even when Angus once ripped his trouser bottoms to shreds. Also, he laughed rather than rang for the police when I ran my hand through my hair and the bleached bit of it snapped off in my hand.

Snogging skills: You're telling me. Well, you *are* telling me because it is so long since I snogged him that I have almost forgotten. I remember his ear-nibbling technique being surprisingly good. Or was that Dave the Laugh? Oy get off this list, Dave the Laugh, you are not on it. This is not "just a good mates" list.

Sense of humor: Generally good. Although I don't think it extends to his songwriting skills. As I have said before, "Oh No It's Me Again," about van Gogh cutting his ear off, is one of the most depressing songs ever written. And believe me, I know, Dad has played me "Agadoo" too often for me not to know what a depressing song is like.

Personality: Yes. I think so. Yes. Again, though, as Dave the Laugh says, you can't entirely trust someone who wears rubber shoes because they don't believe in leather.

Caring: He is nice to Angus and Libby, which are tough darts. So I think he probably scores about an eight.

Minus points.

Hmmmmm.

Well there *is* the aforementioned obsession with the planet, wombats etc. There is definitely a touch of the Jas about him. And, to be frank, he did once choose wombats over me, so once bitten twice whatsit.

Then of course there is the Wet Lindsay factor. It cannot be ignored that his lips have made contact with bits of Old Slimey's anatomy. He did officially go out with her. I really have no excuse for that. And even now he has not given her the severe mental thrashing that she so richly deserves.

But the major minus point is that I don't know if he just wants me for a matey-mate or as a prospective girlfriend.

What I really need is someone to discuss this with. If it was all alrighty with Dave the Laugh, I would deffo ask for his Hornmeister opinion.

one minute later
Actually why isn't it alrighty with Dave the Laugh? He didn't seem at all bothered when he saw me with Robbie. He even asked him to go play pool with him. In anybody's language that is a matey-mate type person and not a prospective snoggee, so I could ask him. I think that is what I will do.

one minute later
Although I don't feel I can just call him and ask him ad hoc and willy-nilly because of his girlfriend situation, so maybe I can get him on his own at the gig tomorrow night and ask him then.
Good plan.
Now I have got all excited in my brain box. I will never sleep I . . .
Zzzzzzzzzzzzzzzzzzz.

the piddly diddly department of life

saturday july 23rd
9:00 a.m.
Is it too soon to start getting ready yet?
Phoned Jas.
She is not even up yet.

9:30 a.m.
None of the ace gang are up. How lazy can you be???
Maybe I will take a quick morning jog over the back fields to get the old corpuscles flinging themselves around in my body.

10:15 a.m.
This is quite pleasant out here in the elements. My little stripey chums the bees are buzzing about in the flowers. Even now at home in the hive the queen bee might be ripping some drone's trouser-snake addendas off. It's a lovely thought. Or two queen bees might be having a bitch fight. Or per-

148

haps all of them are just humming a merry song together, knitting stripey jumpers.

Jog, jog, jog, not too bouncy, keep the nungas flexed so that they don't hit me in the eye and jog, jog, jog. Oh look, there is Mr. Next Door and Mrs. Next Door walking the Prat Poodles. They throw them the stick and off they go yapping after it. They are a ludicrous waste of space really . . . and the poodles are no better! Hahahahaha I have made an inner joke. I'd better get as many inner jokes out of the way as possible before tonight because if there is one thing I have learned it is not to let my brain run free and wild. All sorts of rubbish will come out of my mouth.

I jogged past the Next Doors and waved cheerily to them. They looked a bit alarmed. What is the matter with them? What possible harm can I do them in my running shorts?

11:00 a.m.
I'm just going to go to the edge of the woods and then back home. It's about 11:00 a.m. now, so I could start my steam and cleanse routine. Deep-condition hair at the same time. Then a spot of lunch lovingly prepared by my mother. (Oh I've just accidentally

made another inner joke.) After lunch, a lie-down with cucumber slices and face mask till my lunch has been munched up by the billions of germs and enzymes lurking around my body. They'd better do something to repay me for lugging them about all the time. That would bring the time to about 2:30, long luxurious bath with Mum's special unguents and a very thorough going-over in the mirror for any orangutan genes. I plucked my eyebrows the day before yesterday so I should just about be alright, although those dangly squiggly ones seem to sprout in minutes. Spring out of the bath about 5:00 and then have a bit of a dash to get makeup done by 6:30.

one minute later
Jog, jog.

I might have to cut short my bath just to be on the safe side because if something goes wrong makeupwise . . . you know, dodgy eyeliner or stab in the eye with the mascara brush . . . I'll need extra time to cope.

in the bath
4:00 p.m.
Oh how relaxing is this? Not, is the answer! Dad is

driving me insane with his "Can I possibly get into the bathroom this side of the grave!!" shouting through the keyhole–type stuff.

I am sure he just lounges around waiting for me to have a bath so that he can come and annoy me. He's been doing DIY this arvie so he's bound to be off to casualty in a minute and then at least I will get some peace. Why is he so daddish about doing stuff that he is hopeless at? Mum wanted the kitchen painted and he has insisted that he and Uncle Eddie can do it. It was only a minute and a half before he accidentally painted over the chopping board.

in the kitchen
4:15 p.m.
Dad and Uncle Eddie are almost entirely buttercup yellow. They look like they have had a paint fight.

two minutes later
The kitchen looks like it has had a paint fight.
Mum just looked at me.
I looked at her.
I said, "You chose him."
And I went off to my boudoir. It just shows you

how vair vair careful you must be when you are choosing your partner. She should have made Dad fill out a questionnaire with questions like: Are you sane? And how are your DIY skills? For instance, can you mend a bike wheel without getting your hand stuck and having to go to casualty?

And if the person (Dad) said "no" to both questions, then you run like the wind.

Etc.

Mind you as I said to Mum, I wouldn't even have had to bother with the questionnaire as a quick glance at his enormous conk would have been a deciding factor for me.

in my bedroom

I had almost forgotten about my nose until Miss Octopushead mentioned it again. Let me see.

looking in the mirror

Well it's not small, that is a fact. But providing I don't do any ad hoc smiley smiley without reining my nostrils in I think it could pass for almost normal. I don't know why, perhaps my face has grown around it a bit.

7:10 p.m.
I am ready. Well, as ready as I will ever be.

My makeup went well and I have applied anti-snogging sealant to my lips, although not to my eyes this time. I decided on my short blue dress in the end, with ankle boots. My hair is not bad for once, it has bounceability and umph.

7:15 p.m.
Phoned Jas.

"Jas, are you ready?"

"Yeah, are you? Tom is walking there with Robbie so I'll meet you and the gang at the clock tower if you like."

"Okey diddly dokey. I'm a bit nervy, I hope I don't have a spaz attack on the way there."

"Please don't, the last time you did my tights got laddered when we crashed into the postbox."

7:40 p.m.
Clock tower.

The ace gang rides again!!!

Rosie was all in black, as was Sven. Also Sven was wearing a cowboy hat. He said, "*Ciao* baby, *hasta la vista*."

What fresh hell.

Rosie said, "He's gorgeous, isn't he, my fiancé."

I said, "Er . . . yeah"

Ellen, Jools, Mabs, Honor, Soph (trainee ace gang members), Jas and me walked along chatting together whilst Sven and Rosie brought up the rear (oo-er). There was a big queue outside the Old Market, but Sven swanned up to the front and chatted to the bloke on the door. Oh brilliant, we would probably be banned before we even got in. But to my amazement the bloke said, "Come straight through, girls," and ushered us in. Right past Wet Lindsay and her pals. Yesssssssss!!! She was as livid as a livid thing.

stiff dylans gig

Inside it was already rammed. The Dylans have built up a massive following, it is going to be vair tiring constantly going out as I will have to when I am Masimo's girlfriend. I still can't believe it, actually. You know when you dream about something for so long and then it happens.

one minute later

Well, maybe going to happen if I choose him over

Robbie. Unless Masimo really is two-timing me with Lindsay, and Robbie is only my mate. In which case I am a fool and a loser.

9.30 p.m.
I am sooooo hot and full of tensionosity. Masimo has smiled at me from the stage, but I haven't actually spoken to him. And also, he has smiled at quite a few girls. I have been having a laugh, but also don't quite know what is going on. Ro Ro came up.

"OK, gang, this is a fast one. We could practice the Viking bison dance. Have you all got your horns?"

I said, "Oh drat I forgot mine, never mind, you lot carry on."

Ro Ro looked at me. "Don't you luuuuurve the Viking bison dance? Don't you want me to have a happy wedding?"

I said, "Yes, I do, but as I have another eighteen years to practice the dance before you get married, I am not too bothered."

Rosie said, "Have it your own way, I can't stand chatting to you all night, I have my fiancé to snog."

And she went and hurled herself on Sven and

snogged him right in front of everyone, and he was eating a packet of peanuts at the time.

forty-fifth visit to the tarts' emporium
Lippy still nice and pink and glossy. Which isn't surprising, as I haven't exactly been living in Snog City.

I was just doing a bit of nunga-nunga adjusting and pouting practice when I noticed a little head bobbling about behind me. Then it was joined by another little red head. Two little heads bobbling about behind me. The little titches from school. What were they doing here? Also, they were covered in makeup, they looked like Martha and Minnie the daft vampire twits. (Whoever they are.)

I turned round and said, "What are you two doing here?"

Titch No. 1 said, "We like a bop on a Saturday night."

Are they insane? They are only about twelve. Then I noticed their skirts. Or not, as it happens. They were wearing what looked like belts. I said that to them, I said, "You seem to have come out without your skirts on. It's not PE, you know."

They both started shuffling their legs.

"It's fashion, Miss."

Fashion? Miss? Hang on a minute, I had become my vati!!!

ten minutes later

I gave them a stiff talking-to about the birds and the bees. Well the bees anyway, I told them about the bee arse thing etc. But I also said that Wet Lindsay was here and that if she saw them they were definitely in for an ear-bashing and possibly another visit to the elephant house, or Slim's study, as some fools call it.

They looked a bit frightened. And one said, "We just wanted some fun. We are never allowed to do anything, it's like being in prison. My dad shouts at me when I am on the phone, or in the bathroom or use his razor and everything."

I was nodding along. "I know, I know, I know. Yep I know."

They are very young to know the tragicosity of life, but there you are. Anyway I told them that if they stood in the dark near the bar they could watch the band for another half an hour but then they must go home.

Strangely they seem to think I know what I am

talking about and do what I say. It's a bit like having a couple of ginger retrievers in makeup.

back in the gig
I took the titches to a space behind the bar where it was really dark and left them there all giggly. Wet Lindsay and her tragic mates were "grooving about" (or pratting about, as some might call it) at the far end of the club by the stage. Masimo didn't seem to be paying any attention to her. But then he hadn't paid any attention to me either, other than smiling at me.

fifteen minutes later
The band had done one cracking set. No sign of Robbie yet. Masimo was a fabby singer and his dancing was grooviness personified. All the twittish girls at the front were going mental. I wouldn't be surprised if they started throwing their knickers at him. Very very shaming, they have no pridenosity.

I turned to Jas and said, "You wouldn't fling your knickers on stage, would you Jazzy?"

She said, "Well not the inner ones."

Is she completely insane? Does she actually wear two pairs of knickers? Outer ones and inner ones? I was just about to make her let me have a look when a sort of scuffle-type thing took place by the bar. Oh great, I might have known, the Blunderboys had turned up and Mark Big Gob was having a go at someone.

Ellen and the rest of the gang wanted to go and see what was happening so we went over.

one minute later

Wow and wow and wowzee wow. It was like the shoot-out at the OK Corral. Dave the Laugh and his mates were sizing up to the Blunderboys. Apparently one of the Blunderers had been hitting on the titches, twanging their bra straps and trying to snog them and Dave had noticed and stepped up.

Mark Big Gob said, "Pick a window, you're leaving."

And the next thing I knew, Dave the Laugh was sitting on Mark Big Gob's head.

two minutes later

The bouncers chucked the Blunders out. They are so pathetico, they were yelling, "Watch your back, mate, we know where you live."

Dave said, "Yeah, but do you know where *you*

live, that is the point, you twit."

As they left, Mark did that putting two fingers to his eyes and then pointing them at Dave and then doing a pretend cutting his throat. Amazingly naff.

The titches went up to Dave all mooney and he said, "Home, girls, now, quick as you like."

And they said, "OK, Dave."

And left all girly.

Blimey.

I said to Dave, "They luuurve you."

Dave looked at me. "I am, it has to be said, Jack the Biscuit."

Then he puckered up and did a really mad fast twisting dance. He was shouting, "Just call me Big Dave!!!"

I was laughing when Emma came over with a drink for him. She said "hi" to me and then gave him a kiss and a hug. Weird. Well, the kiss and the hug weren't weird, but it made me feel sort of weird.

I sloped off to the ace gang.

break

Robbie arrived. Wet Lindsay must have been on high

alert because he had only just got through the door before she flung herself on him and took him to the bar. God, I hate her. I must say he didn't look too thrilled to see her and he was looking around. Maybe he was looking for me. I had a sudden spaz attack and said to Jas, "Jas, I am going to hide behind you, don't move, I want to see what is going on."

Jas is useless as camouflage, she keeps forgetting her role and every time she says anything to me she turns round to talk to me and reveals me crouching down behind her. What is the point in that?

Lindsay was being all "animated," if an octopus can be animated. Robbie was being polite, but he looked a bit distracted. The he saw the Dylans coming from backstage to the bar and said something to Lindsay and went over to speak to them. As he turned his back on her, Lindsay reached down the front of her top and did a bit of adjusting. Ah-hah, her false basoomas must have come free from their lashings. Good.

The Dylans sat down at a table and were immediately surrounded by girls all fluffing and farting about. Jas said, "I'm going to the bar with Tom, you'll have to fend for yourself."

I said, "Jas, Jazzy, don't leave me, just walk

slowly across to the bar and I will lurk behind you."

So I shuffled over to the bar behind her, but just as we got almost opposite the Dylans' table, she bumped into Sven. Oh no. Sven could see me sort of lurking behind Jas and he said, "Aha!!! Let us groove baby, Sven likes to groove."

And he picked me up and started doing this sort of jive-type dance, only my feet were not touching the ground. It was horrific and I am pretty sure you could see my knickers and therefore my tights. Which must have looked really erm . . . crap.

I said, "Put me down, Sven, please."

Eventually he lost interest in me because Rosie came up in her bison horns and said, "I feel the Horn coming on."

And Sven put me down on a table. The Dylans' table. The table that both Masimo and Robbie were sitting at. Oh marvelous.

My bottom was inches away from a Sex God and a Luuurve God.

What would a person full of sophisticosity and maturiosity say?

I said, "Anyone know the footie results?"

Oh no, I had *déjà* whatsit. I slipped off the table and everyone looked at me.

Masimo half-smiled and said, "Miss Georgia, I hope you have not a train to catch tonight."

And he and all the lads laughed. I of course went beetroot. Thank God it was so dark.

I shambled off to the tarts' wardrobe.

As I went past her, Wet Lindsay put her face really near mine and said quietly, "Did the little girl make a fool of herself in front of the big boys? Diddums."

tarts' wardrobe

All the ace gang assembled.

Mabs said, "You sat on their table?"

Jools said, "You asked about the footie? Again?"

Rosie said, "Did you say you had to catch a train?"

Ellen said, "I mean, you could see, erm, your . . . knickers."

Jas said, "I bet you wished you had my big knickers on now."

back in the club of life

On the way back from the loo, I bumped into Dave. He smiled at me in his groovy way and said, "Ah,

Sex Kitty, have you just been to the piddly diddly department?"

I said in a dignitosity-at-all-times way, "Er no, I certainly haven't . . ."

He said, "Ah . . . so it was the poo parlor division, then?"

Oh it was sooo nice to see him. We both laughed. He looked at me from underneath his eyelashes for a bit. He has got really nice eyes, smiley and sexy at the same time. I wonder if I should . . .

And then he said, "I'm just off for a wazz."

I said really quickly, "Dave, can I ask you a question in your capacity as official Hornmeister? What do you think Robbie thinks about me? I mean, do you know anything? You know, any boy-type signs that I might not know about?"

He looked at me again, and then he looked over to where his girlfriend was talking to her mates. She waved at him and he waved back. He said, "Well, I think that Robbie does like you, but he is not sure where he stands and he doesn't know what is going on with Masimo, so he is playing it near to his chest and cool bananas."

I love Dave the Laugh.

But only in a, you know, matey way.

Then we saw Masimo coming our way. He was being stopped by girls as he pushed his way through the crowds.

Dave said, "Oy hold up, here comes the Italian Stallion. I hope he is not going to hit me with his handbag because I am talking to you."

I said, "Dave, he hasn't got a handbag."

But Dave still wouldn't leave it alone. He said, "Well I hope he doesn't hit me with his sports bra then."

He really is vair vair annoying.

Masimo came up to us then, and Dave said, "Cracking set. I'm just off to the wazzarium." And he went off.

Masimo said, "He is going to the wazzranium? What is this?"

Oh dear God. I said, "Well it's, you know, like the boys . . . erm . . . piddly diddly . . . no no, forget that. Er, he's gone to the loo."

Masimo smiled. "My English is still, how you say . . . ?"

And I said, "Crapio?"

fifteen minutes later
I am on cloud ninety-five, I think. Masimo is

catching his plane to Italy early in the morning and he said he has to pack up after the gig, but can he meet me and I can go round to his place and see him off. I said yes, but this is going to take some planning. Jas will have a spaz attack if I don't report back to Jas Headquarters like I am supposed to do. So my cunning plan is this. I go home with Jazzy, do pretendy going to bed, slip out of her house when everyone has gone to bed (using Jas's key, which she will lend me) and meet Masimo for a few hours. Then he drops me back at Jas's in time for me to do pretendy getting up after a good night's sleep.

All I have to do now is to explain to Jas what an excellent plan it is.

Perhaps I could just hit her over the head with a particularly heavy owl and sneak out.

11:45 p.m.
How cool!! Robbie joined in with the last two songs of the gig. We are all dancing like loons. But loons that have sophisticosity and whatsit. It was fabby having two singers, they sounded really groovy together. I don't know why we can't have a *ménage à trois* actually. . . . Everyone does in *la belle* France.

midnight

Getting our coats. Robbie strolled over and said, "Alright, girls?"

Then he smiled at me. "I haven't had much chance to talk to you, Georgia, do you need a lift home?"

Oh Blimey O'Reilly's trousers . . . he really did have dreamy blue eyes, really dark blue like a dark blue sea or like a . . . hang on a minute, my lips were puckering up without my permission!! Stop it, stop it!!!

I said, "Well I'm staying at Jas's, but . . ."

At which point in unusually crap timing even for her, the creature from the lagoon, Wet Lindsay, came sliming up. She totally *ignorez-vous*ed me and linked up with Robbie and said to him, "How about that drink you promised me?"

Robbie looked at me and I looked at him. Now was the time for me to say, "I need to talk to you." Yeah, that was the thing to do now. But if anyone knows what to do it won't be me. Lindsay said to me, "Bye-bye, don't be late home," and started leading Robbie off. And I just stood there not saying anything.

He turned back and said, "Maybe another time, Georgia?"

Wet Lindsay turned back as well and gave me the evils.

What a prizewinning cow she is.

five minutes later

I was still spluttering about her. "What a slimey octopussy cow she is!! She made Robbie have a drink with her. He said, 'Do you want a lift home, Georgia?' and there she was like the bride of a jellyfish, lurking and sliming about."

Rosie said, "We must eat her; it's the only solution."

As we left the club, Masimo was packing up on the stage and he shouted to me, "*Ciao*, Georgia, see you soon."

And all the girls who had been hovering around looked over at me and THEY gave me the evils. If I was a voodoo doll I'd be covered in pins from head to foot.

I waved back in a casualosity-at-all-times way. Ooooh I don't know what to think.

Ellen started dithering for England, "Er, what,

why did he ... I mean, what does he mean 'see you soon'?"

I said, "Well I am going round to his house later."

Rosie said, "I thought you were staying at Jas's?"

I said, "Well I am in principle, but then I am going to sneak out and he will pick me up at the end of Jas's road."

Jools said, "Blimey."

I said, "I know. Pizza-a-gogo-type snogging for me. I'll let you know if he does any unexpected tongue work."

Mabs said, "How has Jas explained it to her mum and dad? There's no way I could get out of my house without the flying squad being called."

I said, "Oh, well they are cool with it."

They all looked at me.

Rosie said, "You haven't told Jas, have you?"

"Well, not as such."

Rosie said, "She will have a nervy b. and probably pop off to Strop Central."

God, life is complicated. As I said to Rosie, "This is what comes of being too likeable."

She said, "Who?"

"Me."

She did that slapping me on both cheeks thing she does and said, "Don't be mad."

walking home with the gang
I made them shut up about my night visit to Luuurve land when Jas and Tom came and joined us to walk home.

four minutes later
I think I might be in a good mood. Because a Luuurve God in the hand is worth two on the bus, and I am meeting up with a Luuurve God later even if a Sex God has gone off on the bus . . . anyway, you get my drift.

I am even in the mood to join in with the mad ramblings of Radio Jas. She was all snuggled up with Tom as we ambled along, and every now and again they would stop and have a little kiss. Not full-on snogging, but just a pecky affair. Sweet, really. If you like that sort of thing.

Just then there was a mad ringing of a bell fiasco and Sven came riding up on a child's bike.

"Hi girls, rock and roll!!!!"

And he did a wheelie before crashing into a tree. Then he just left the bike on the ground and got hold of Rosie and put her over his shoulder. You could see her knickers. Sven said, "I am a wild and crazy guy!!!"

He's not wrong there. Rosie said from upside down, "Tatty bye! Sven and I are going to snog for a bit."

And he peeled off into the park. With his hump/girlfriend.

Ellen and Jools and Mabs and Honor were all being taken home by Mabs's dad. She had made him park two streets away from the market in case anyone saw him. And also as a double precaution he had to pretend to be reading a newspaper so that none of her friends could see his head. You see they say that teenagers show no initiative and so on, but we are constantly having to think about this sort of thing. It is vair vair tiring.

After we'd said s'laters to everybody, Jas and Tom and I continued on to her place. Tom said, "Good gig, wasn't it? He's a cool guy, Masimo. Don't you think so, Gee?"

It is a bit awkward for me being completely honest around Tom, him being Robbie's brother and so on.

I sort of mumbled something.

Jas said, "Yeah, do you think he is cool, Georgia?" and looked at me in a meaningful way. I didn't say anything so she opened her eyes really wide and raised her eyebrows. I raised my eyebrows back at her. We could have gone on doing that all night, but then Tom said, "So have you had 'the talk' with my bro?"

I said, "Well, erm, not really. He went off with Lindsay."

Tom said, "Yeah well, I wouldn't exactly call it that, she sort of made him take her for a drink, that isn't the same as him asking her for a drink."

I decided to take the bull by the legs and hurl it about a bit and strap a little hat on its head and . . . shut up, brain. I decided to ask Tom what he thought was going on.

I said, "Has Robbie said anything about what he thinks about me?"

Tom shuffled about a bit and said, "Well, he's always said how much he liked you, and that he was really sorry that it didn't work out between you . . . and that it was, like, more or less just to do with the fact that he thought you were a bit . . . well, young for him."

Jas said, "She is too young for him, she's too

young for anyone, actually. . . ."

I looked at her and said, "Oh thanks, besty pal."

She was in Wise Mavis of the Woods mood though, she should get a stick and grow a beard. Ramble ramble. "I am just being realistic, Gee, you are not a serious sort of person, you are giddy, you like snot dancing and so on, you are not ready for a proper relationship, you just want to blow your horn and so on. That is just *le* fact."

I didn't know what to say to that. Perhaps she is right. Perhaps I am a hollow sham of a person who will end up on my own in a cellar. Or as the coowner of a corduroy shop with Miss Wilson.

It made me feel a bit miz. Not as miz as I felt ten minutes later when I had to hang around the garage like a goosegog whilst Jas and Tom kissed good night. I wasn't allowed to go into the house because Jas said we had to go into the house together. I would have ignored her, but I still hadn't broken the news about my early morning Snog Fest. I tried not to notice them, but I could sort of hear them snogging. Squelchy noises and breathing and rustling. It was like being a pervy. In fact I had become the female equivalent of Elvis Attwood. Bloody hell.

four years later

Eventually Jas dragged herself away from Tom and after about ninety-five years of her saying "Bye, then," and then rushing after him for one last kiss I managed to get her through the door.

jas's house

Jas's mum came into the kitchen in her (sensible) nightie. No suggestion of nungas akimbo like there would have been round at my house. She said, "Did you have a good time, girls? I have left some snacks out for you, you must be ravenous. I'm off to bed. I made the bed all snuggly for you. Night, God bless."

And she went off. Amazing. No third degree. No "And who did you dance with, was there any snogging?" from Mum or "What bloody time do you call this, you treat this house like a bloody hotel" from Dad. Just some snacks and good night.

Quite, quite amazing.

upstairs

Jas was ages in the bathroom. What is she doing in there?

I said through the door, "Jas, what are you doing in there?"

She said, "I am applying nighttime moisturizer."

Good Lord. She must have used a bucket of it by now.

in bed

I am fully dressed.

Jas said, "Georgia, you are fully dressed."

"I know, I am going out in a minute."

She said, "What???"

I said, "Yes I told you, I am being picked up by Masimo at one a.m. He is setting off to the airport at three a.m. so I should be back about then."

She said, "You did not tell me you were meeting Masimo, but it doesn't matter because you are not meeting him. That is a fact."

"Jazzy."

"And anyway, what about Robbie? What have you told him? What will he think about it? Anyway, he won't think anything about it because you're not meeting Masimo."

"Jazzy."

"No, if you get caught I will be grounded for years."

"Yes, but Jazzy, I will not be caught, I will just do creepy creep out of the back door using your key, creepy creep down to the bottom of the street, be picked up by my gorgey fabby Luuurve God, snog, chat, snog, chat, maybe do a bit of quiet crying as he says *arrivederci*. But not enough crying to spoil my eye makeup. And also I will be seeing him quite soon when I go on my holiday to Rome."

Jas was having a massive tizz and hump, even for her.

"This is so typical of you. If anyone gets into trouble it will be me, and you probably won't do creepy creep, you'll probably fall over something and wake everyone up and even if you do get back into the house you will go into the wrong bedroom or something."

I gave her a big hug.

"Don't you want me to be happy, Jazzy?"

"No."

That's nice, isn't it?

I said, "Look, I'll do a practice creep now, I'll creep into the kitchen and see if you can hear me."

12:30 a.m.

I can't believe this. Jas made such a fuss about me

making a noise, but by the time I got back from creeping around she had fallen asleep!!!

There is a similarity between Jas's house and mine, her vati and mutti both snore. Which is good because it means they are asleep.

12:50 a.m.

I wonder what it will be like being with Masimo? For two hours? All aloney with the Luuurve God. Or maybe Dom, his flat mate, will be there and we won't get time to snog. *Sacré bleu!*

in the bathroom

I look OK. I don't know whether to do just lip gloss because of the maybe snognosity of the situation, or to rely on the lip sealant stuff and do full lippy.

Ohhhh I don't know.

12:55 a.m.

Time to girdey the loins and pucker up.

Crept downstairs and into the kitchen . . . I had already opened the back door so that I wouldn't make any noise at all. Stepped out into the back garden. Stars all twinkling about in the sky. Looking down on me like twinkly, erm, twinkly things.

I know that I had said they were useless, like sort of dim blinky torches, but now I could see that they were jolly. Like tiny jolly lights, lighting my way to a snogathon. That's how good a mood I was in.

Vair vair good.

1:05 a.m.

Sitting on a garden wall at the end of Jas's street.

Brr, it's a bit nippy noodles even though it is the middle of summer. And a bit quiet and creepy.

Maybe he won't come? Maybe he was talking to the rest of the Stiff Dylans about me and they said, "Are you mad, mate?" Or maybe his ex-girlfriend phoned up and they have decided to get back together, or . . .

And that's when I heard his scooter approaching.

I stood up. Then I sat down again. What would a cool person do? Would they stand up or sit down in a casualosity-at-all-times sort of way? I wish I smoked, at least I would have something in my hand. Although with my luck, I would probably set fire to my head. I know what, I could be looking through my bag and just look up when he got to me.

I started rustling about in my bag as the scooter got nearer. Then he was there. I looked up and he was sitting on his scooter. He took his helmet off and shook his hair loose. Good grief and jelloid leggies akimbo. He was quite literally gorgeous. And he had actually come to see me. For once I just felt sooooo happy to be me. And lucky. I was in love with the world. Yes, even Jazzy. The whole wide world. Apart from Wet Lindsay.

Masimo smiled and said, *"Ciao, caro,"* and blew me a kiss. Then he got the spare helmet and patted the seat behind him. "Come, let us ride."

It was like being in a film. He even put the helmet on for me and as he fastened the chin strap he kissed me on the lips. I really did nearly fall over. Then he said to me, "Are you OK, safe? Hold on to me."

I put my hands on his waist. Blimey, touching him was like getting an electric shock. Beam me up, Scotty, as they say in one of those TV things that boys like so much, full of people from other planets with weird heads like cauliflowers. Why do boys like things that look so weird—hobbits and elves and mekons and so on? I don't know and I don't care because I have got a Luuuurve God in my hands who hasn't got a cauliflower for a head. And who LIKES me!!!

Yessssssss!!! I had a song in my heart, and it was not "Funky Moped" by Jasper Carrott.

We drove through the dark streets, it was absolutely fabby. There were still a few people coming home from clubs singing and dancing around. We pulled up at a traffic light and Masimo said, "I thought we would go to my place and I can give you Italian coffee . . . and other Italian things."

Blimey O'Reilly's trousers. At this rate, I wouldn't be able to get off the bike for jelloidness.

1:30 a.m.

Masimo's flat is cool. He shares it with Dom and a mate of Dom's. It's quite tidy and there is no undercrackers pile like in Mum and Dad's room. I wonder what sort of undercrackers Masimo wears? Italian-type ones. Maybe musical ones that play "Arrivederci Roma" or "Nessun Dorma." No, no Masimo would never wear novelty under-crackers . . . Why have I wandered into the under-wear department?

Masimo has made me proper coffee in a machine-type thing, with some little biscuits that taste of almond. I feel *très* European. As I sipped my coffee, he finished his packing. He had some cool shirts.

When he finished he shut his case and looked at me. "So, Miss Georgia, does Robbie know about us?"

I looked at him. "Well, he . . . I . . ."

Masimo put his arms around me. "Perhaps I can help you, *caro* . . ."

2:30 a.m.

Crikey, I feel like a dozy bumble bee. Masimo has to be the best snogger ever. He kissed me really slowly for ages without a break. It wasn't even No. 4 (kiss lasting three minutes without a break), it was more like No. 4 times three (a kiss lasting at least a quarter of an hour).

And he talks and stuff. Not whilst we are snogging, because clearly you wouldn't be able to know what he was saying, other than "nnuummppphhhmmmernuummmpphh." But what I mean is the inbetweeny bits, when he'd stop kissing me and then look in my eyes and stroke my hair. Saying stuff like *bellissima* and so on. And for a bit he was running his hands up from the bottom of my throat to

181

my lips and then putting his fingers just slightly in my mouth. Gadzooks! It was fabby. Apparently girls are supposed to have about two hundred thousand million more sensory nerves than boys. We are pleasure machines!!!

Masimo seemed to like it just as much as me.

2:50 a.m.
Masimo looked up at the clock. "Oh my God, my plane. I so, do not, want to leave you, Georgia, I wish I could stay here all night with you. I really like you. Please will you come and visit with me? I don't want to wait for a month to see you. Will you try?"

I tried to sit up and get my lips under control. They felt like they had swollen to about fourteen times their normal size. Masimo was speaking in Pizza-a-gogo land talk as he made sure he had his passport and tickets. Ummmm, how groovy does he sound? The fact that he was probably saying "Buggeration, where's my sodding pants?" didn't matter because he was speaking the language of luuurve. Not just some crap foreign language.

Like German. It wouldn't have sounded at all the same in Lederhosen talk. "*I zink du bist ein*

gutten looken fraulein. Du bist wunderbar like *ze*
big *spangleferkel. Ich vant* to frontal *knutschen*
you!!! *Oh ja oh jah!!!*"

Whilst my brain had been off to Loonland,
Masimo had got his stuff together.

He grabbed his coat and then as he was
putting it on, got hold of me and pulled me toward
him. He smelled sooooo nice, sort of him and a
perfume thing all mixed up. He kissed me very
hard on the lips for a long time and then put both
of his hands round my head and looked me in the
eyes. "We like each other, it will be good, Miss
Georgia."

The doorbell rang and it was the cab.

We bundled in the cab and carried on snogging
and within seconds it seemed like we were at Jas's
corner and I had to get out and leave him.
Noooooooooooooo. I think I am in luuuuurve. . . .

Masimo kissed me again and looked really sad.
"I will miss you."

I got out in a sort of daze and waved to him as
the cab pulled away.

And then I realized that I actually *was* crying.
Real tears. Not pretend tears. My heart felt really
soft and full and sad. It all seemed like a dream. I

could still feel his kisses on my mouth.

I will never ever be able to sleep tonight. I don't want to, I want to remember this forever. I walked around the back of the house. It was a beautiful night with a deep black sky and I could hear the soft hooting of an owl in the distance. Normally I would have been annoyed but tonight I thought "Good night, Mr. Owl, I hope you have a Mrs. Owl at home to keep you company . . . unless you are in fact a Mrs. Owl and then I hope you have a Mr. Owl at home, and if you don't you could always join Jas in her bed if you like stuffed owls, that would be a hoot."

Yes, it is official, I am actually telling jokes to owls. I must be in love.

I let myself in the back door and crept up the stairs of the silent house and into Jas's room. There she was all curled up with her arm around Snowy Owl. Hmmmm. Well, live and let live, I say. I got undressed and settled down among my friends the owls.

blah, blah, rubbish, rubbish, dribble, dribble, dribble, arse!

sunday july 24th
woke up at the crack of 9:30 a.m.

Jas was still snoozing on her side of the bed. I forgot where I was for a minute, but then I remembered everything that had happened. Oooohhhhhh Masimo. I was missing him already. He would be in Rome by now. I wonder if he was thinking about me.

Because I love the world so much, I may go down and ask Jas's mum if I can have a cup of tea for me and my little fringey matey.

Went downstairs. There was no one around. On the kitchen unit was a note that said:

Dear Jas,
We are out on a bit of a ramble, we have
our flasks so may be gone for the day.
There are eggs and stuff for brekky and I
thought you and Georgia might like a pizza

later so I have left you some money. Have
a lovely day.
Lots of love
Mum

Wow. Now that is PROPER hands-off parenting. Just leaving food and buggering off. Top. I made some tea and even boiled a little eggy for Jas, because I know how much she loves eggs. I put it on a tray and went into her bedroom.

I put the tray on the bedside table and leaned over Jas. I got one of the smaller owls and made it kiss her with its little beak. She shot up in bed and was all surly and her fringe was standing on end like an electrocuted hedgehog.

"What have you done? Did you get caught coming in?"

I told Jas that her m and d had gone out rambling and then I said, "Do you want to know all that happened with me and my new boyfriend the Luuurve God?"

She said, "No."

But I knew she wanted to know, really.

in my bedroom

4:00 p.m.

So that was it. It is official news because I have told Radio Jas that Masimo is my new boyfriend. I've been into the cakeshop, I've dithered about for a bit, but I've finally chosen the Italian fancy.

How many hours was it since I had last snogged him? I have already got snogging withdrawal and that is *le* fact.

Phoned Rosie.

"Ro Ro, have you ever had your neck stroked by Sven?"

"Only when he is wearing his gardening gloves. Why?"

"Well it's just that Masimo did it last night, it was fab. Also we did number four, but it was times four."

At that point my vati came looming unexpectedly out of the front room and said, "What is number four?"

My dad had accidentally entered my snogging space. Erlack. I just looked at him and said, "This is a private conversation, actually, Dad."

5:30 p.m.

Uncle Eddie arrived. I scampered upstairs before he could tell me any "jokes."

I must try and distract myself from thinking about Masimo. I will do something that I can really get involved in.

6:30 p.m.

I must get some eyelash curlers. Everyone in *CosmoGirl* uses them.

7:00 p.m.

Doorbell rang.

Now it's some of Mum's aerobics mates coming round. I wonder why. They normally only come round if there are firemen here.

7:30 p.m.

Oh please let that not be Abba playing.

8:00 p.m.

Libby is singing along to "Dancing Bean."

8:30 p.m.

What are they doing down there? All I can hear is

helpless laughing from Mum and Libby. And really crap loud music. With the occasional bang like someone has fallen over.

9:30 p.m.

Things are not getting any better, in fact they are getting worserer. I have never heard so much laughing and squealing. What are they doing down there?

9:40 p.m.

OK, I have had it. They are playing that song from *The Full Monty*—what is it called, when the blokes at the end take off their uniforms and dance about in their nuddy-pants. *You Can Leave Your Hat On*, it's called. And all Mum's mates are catcalling and yelling, "Get them off!!" I am going to have to tell them to be quiet.

9:45 p.m.

When I opened the living room door, Uncle Eddie was waggling his bottom around to the music. In his undercrackers.

midnight

I will definitely have to go into the priory for

counseling. Uncle Eddie is going to be a stripper. Honestly. You know when you can order a policeman or a fireman or a James Bond–o-gram for a hen night or a birthday? Well apparently, and I cannot imagine the kind of people this involves, there is a demand for a baldy-o-gram. And Uncle Eddie is going to be it.

Grown-ups are absolutely obsessed with sex. It's horrific.

12:35 a.m.

Libby has seen a baldy bloke in his undercrackers. She will certainly be scarred for life and end up with a phobia about boiled eggs.

It all adds up. Dad dying his hair, the leather trousers, the prancing around like a loon. He is having a midlife crisis even though in my opinion his life is two-thirds over.

12:40 a.m.

So if Vati cannot be relied upon to be a proper dad, I must take responsibility myself.

12:45 a.m.

This does not mean I will be growing a little beard.

monday july 25th
morning
I have written a "Dad's book of rules" and posted it under Mum and Dad's bedroom door.

This is what it says:

DAD RULES.

DO NOT ASK ME WHO I AM MEETING.

IF I ALLOW YOU TO DROP ME OFF SOME-WHERE IN YOUR "CAR," DO NOT EVER ROLL DOWN THE WINDOW AND SHOUT SOME-THING AFTER ME. EVEN THOUGH I WILL PRETEND I CAN'T HEAR YOU, SOME OF MY FRIENDS MIGHT HEAR YOU.

DON'T GIVE ME MONEY IN FRONT OF EVERYONE.

NEVER ENTER MY ROOM UNASKED (YOU WILL NEVER BE ASKED).

DO NOT SNOG IN FRONT OF ME AND LIBBY OR MY FRIENDS OR ANYONE. OR BETTER STILL, DO NOT SNOG. THERE IS NO NEED FOR IT AT YOUR AGE.

WEAR PROPER DAD TROUSERS.

BAN UNCLE EDDIE, OR THE BALDY-O-GRAM MAN, FROM OUR HOUSE. THE VISION OF HIM IN HIS COMEDY UNDERCRACKERS

WILL BE WITH ME TO THE GRAVE.
THANK YOU.
GEORGIA

8:10 a.m.

I scampered out of the house before anyone was moving around. I heard a lot of moaning from the bedroom, which serves everyone right. As Romulus or Remus or Ethelred the Unready says (anyway, one of the clever dick philosopher types), "Ye cannot have your fun and eat it." Elderly men should learn to leave off the *vino tinto* and keep their pants on.

10:30 a.m.
careers talk

Miss Wilson is in charge because Hawkeye is off girl-baiting (she says on a course, but we know what she does really). So the career talk, usually a very dull time, offers many, many comedy opportunities.

Rosie started by saying, "Miss Wilson, what openings might there be in casual work for Viking brides? I am particularly interested in reindeers and vats."

Miss Wilson said, "Rosie, please try and be serious."

Rosie looked puzzled. "I am."

And the sadnosity is that she is telling the truth.

Ellen says she is interested in nursing which is the first I have heard about it. I tell you one thing, I will not be going into any emergency department that has Ellen in it. The last thing you need when your arm is hanging off is to have Ellen saying, "Erm well, is it your left arm or, erm, do you or something, or is it the other one?"

ten minutes later

To think she showed us the bee film. Miss Wilson is very ill informed on courses for beekeeping and backing singing.

4:20 p.m.

As I was ambling home with Jools and Rosie, the two little titches came pelting up to me. All keen and red-faced.

"Er, Miss, wasn't it brillo pads at the gig??? Is it the singer one that you like? He's like . . ."

I said, "Brillo pads?"

And they both went, "Yeah!!!"

Like twin mini loons. Then Titch No. 1 said, "But, you know what, I think Dave is the grooviest of them all, I know he's not a pop star or anything, but I think he's lovely."

She went absolutely beetroot.

The second little titch said, "We love him."

And then they ran off.

Blimey. Dave the Laugh has a growing fan club.

teatime at bonkers headquarters

Grandad and Maisie are here. I wasn't allowed to go to my room, but had to sit around listening to madnosity for hours.

Grandad said, "I have an announcement to make. Maisie has just made me the happiest man alive."

I nearly said, *Why, is she going on a knitting tour of the world?* But I didn't. Grandad reached over and took one of Maisies hands (well as much as he could as she was wearing multicolored mittens. Keep in mind this is July).

"She has agreed to marry me."

kitchen
10:00 p.m.

Mum was making some coffee and the "swingers," Grandad and Maisie, had staggered off home.

Mum said, "It just shows you that you must never give up on love; it comes when you least expect it."

I said, "Mum, it is sad and weird."

She said, "I think it's lovely and romantic."

I said, "You won't when you have to wear a knitted jumpsuit for the wedding."

Mum was still in elderly loon land because she said, "Age isn't everything. Grandad says she's a fine body of a woman underneath all that wool."

Erlack a pongoes!

Anyway, who cares about the knitted folk? Is now a good time to get Mum to agree for me to go to Pizza-a-gogo land? I am having very bad withdrawal symptoms from the Luuurve God. I have dreamt about him last night and it was a bit alarming. He had been doing the neck-stroking thing and my neck had started stretching like it was a piece of clay. You know, like when you see those programs about potters making vases and they stretch the clay. Anyway that was happening and then my head fell off.

I think it is probably Freudian. I think it means I mustn't lose my head. Especially as in the dream, my head rolled off into a corner and Angus came and started biffing it around like a ball.

Where was I? Oh yes. Asking Mum when I could go to Pizza-a-gogo land.

"Mum, which do you think would be the best week for me to go to Rome? I finish term next week and then there is the ludicrous camping weekend, but I could go the weekend after that."

She said, "Why are you talking rubbish about going to Italy?"

I laughed in a lighthearted way.

"Oooh Mum, you prankster!!! You know what I mean, I mean about going to visit Masimo's family as we agreed."

"Agreed?"

"Yes."

"Where was I when we agreed?"

"You were, er, near me, agreeing."

"Georgia, A, I did not agree and B, nothing you say will make me agree. And C, the first two—times a million."

five minutes later

I HATE my family. Why do they want me to hang around all the time—why can't they make their own fun??? Well, this time I will show them. If they won't let me have the money to go to Italy to see my boyfriend, then I will get the money myself.

I will sell something.

ten minutes later
Looking through my cupboards.

How much would I get for my slightly worn leather boots? Where do you take stuff to sell it? I don't know. Oxfam? A selling shop?

I like them and anyway, what would I wear in Italy for disco wear?

And also, I am very, very tired. It's the end of term, I have been working like a dog, I haven't got the energy to go traipsing around earning my own money.

midnight
I am going to not speak to my mum and dad until they let me go to see the Luuurve God.

tuesday july 26th
breakfast
Mum asked me if I wanted some toast and I *ignorez-vous*ed her. It won't be long before she snaps.

As I was silently leaving the house, Mum said, "If you are planning to keep up the silent treatment,

I'll just have to guess what you would say. Which is quite handy actually as I want you to babysit tonight. I'm guessing that you want to. Yes yes, I can see you do. That's good. Tatty bye."

Damn!!!

2:00 p.m.

I can't believe I'm being made to go on this camping fiasco. In German, Herr Kamyer showed us a lot of things you can do with a Swiss Army knife. All of them indescribably useless and naff.

I said to Ro Ro, "In my humble opinion, if a horse gets a stone stuck in its hoof, that is just carelessnosity. Why should I have to lug a heavy knife around just so I can get it out?"

Ro Ro gave me the Klingon salute. "You are all heart, Georgia. Do you want to practice a sheepshank knot with me?"

I just looked at her. Jas adores doing sheepshank knots. Please make this camping trip go away, God!

4:15 p.m.

Detention! I can't believe it!!! Hawkeye has only been back about five minutes from her girl-baiting course and she has given me detention.

I was three minutes late for her class because I had to go to the piddly diddly department after German and noticed a lurker situation that I had to deal with by squeezing the living daylights out of it and then covering it with soap. I don't know why, it seemed a good idea at the time. Anyway, when I panted into class, Hawkeye said, "You should have been here at three o'clock."

And I said, "Why? What happened?" in a tone of interest and curiosity. And the next thing you know I am in detention writing "Rudeness masquerading as wittiness results in detention."

Unbelievable.

in my room
6:30 p.m.
Still thinking of ways to get to my beloved. I wonder if he will ring me from Pizza-a-gogo land? I would ring him if I were him. Well, you know what I mean. Mind you, I would have rung me on Monday.

five minutes later
I wonder—why he hasn't phoned me?

I'd phone Jas and ask her what she thinks but

she is in Twig land. If I hear one more thing about this bloody camping trip I will go insane. Also, and this is annoying, Jas would not do sharesies in her tent. She is dossing down with Ellen and Mabs, she says they are more "reliable." What does that mean? I don't care, I am sharing with Rosie and Jools which will be more fun anyway. Jas will have all these stupid "tent rules" like "Toothbrushes should be kept in the toothbrush jar" and "When you go to bed at night, check that your sleeping bag is not crushing some unusual wildlife." Rubbish stuff.

What are you supposed to take clotheswise for a camping nightmare scenario?

We got a list somewhere from Miss Wilson. Where is it?

two minutes later
Warm evening clothing.

A rainproof.

Walking shoes.

Casual daywear.

Good lord. Oh and this is a terrifying bit: "Bring your bathing suits, girls, because there is a river nearby, and of course if you have any instruments that you play, bring those along to make the evenings lots of fun!"

It is going to be a cross between a "Call-Me-Arnold the Vicar guitar extravaganza and "carry on camping." I can guarantee that the mountain rescue people will be called out. It will possibly be something to do with Melanie Griffiths running and her basoomas sending her out of control and into the river. That or Herr Kamyer will be savaged by sheep (with a bit of luck).

7:00 p.m.
Rosie rang.

"Gee, I am taking the horns with us on the camping trip. Pip pip."

I said, "Why?"

She said, "So we can brush up on our Viking disco inferno dance and also we can don them if we are attacked by rampaging cows."

Good grief.

ten minutes later
I suppose in some horrific way the camping fiasco will pass the time until I can figure out how to get to Masimo.

in my room

I wonder how Robbie is. Every time I can't avoid
going near Wet Lindsay she says something about
him to one of her slimey mates, implying that they
are an item. Maybe they are. Well if they are, it is a
good way of curing me of him. Anyone who could
choose someone as nobbly as her can't be all
good.

one minute later

But he did ask me if I wanted a lift home before she
trapped him with her octopussy extensions.

one minute later

And Dave the Laugh said he thought Robbie liked
me, but he was playing cool bananas because of
the Masimo fandango.

one minute later

Oh no, I've been thinking about Dave the Laugh
again. He somehow still pops up! Oo-er. If I think
of anything funny, I always want to tell him about it.
I don't because, well, it seems a bit odd just being
mates with him. It was cool on Saturday night
when he saved the little titches.

I wonder if he laughs with his girlfriend Emma like he laughs with me?

I wonder what number on the snogging scale they have got up to. Shut up, brain.

Phone rang.

Maybe it's Masimo! I ran down the stairs. No one is in because Mum said she'd decided I couldn't be trusted to look after Libbs so she has taken her over to Grandad and his knitted live-in lover. Oh much more trustworthy. Not. I nearly said that to Mum, but it's difficult when you are not speaking to someone. Why can't I have normal parents who do stuff for me? Mum and Dad have gone to Uncle Eddie's first booking as a baldy-o-gram.

And that in anybody's language is not normal behavior.

I answered the phone.

It was Robbie.

Crikey.

three minutes later

I have agreed to meet him on Thursday for a "talk."

Whatever that means.

Well, in my case it will mean me going, "Blah blah, rubbish, rubbish, dribble, dribble, arse."

thursday july 28th
last day of term

Got the "whole school is looking to you for an example" speech from Slim about the camping trip. And she said, "We are all looking forward very much to the interesting stories and observations that Ten A will be coming back with."

Oh yes, the merry hours we will have talking about the night we saw a badger scratch its bumoley. And how many sausages we ate.

As we lurched along to Latin, I said to Rosie, "Why isn't Slim coming with us, actually? I personally would give quite a lot of money to see her in a tent."

Rosie said, "She was wearing one today."

Jas was hysterical with twig madness. "Have you packed yet, Gee?"

"No."

"I have."

"Really, how many pairs of knickers are you bringing?"

"Well I thought just in case of nippy noodles weather I would bring those thick long ones that—"

"Jas, I am not serious."

She huffed off.

She is so self-obsessed it's amazing. It's all just me, me, me, Tom, me, stuffed owls, knickers and er . . . me with her. If you see what I mean and I think you do.

I told her on the way to Stalag 14 this morning that I was on the horns of a whatsit vis-á-vis the maybe-two-boyfriends situation. And I am. I am feeling quite weird about seeing Robbie this evening.

She gave me the usual Jas lecture. "Well, you have to choose and then stick with your decision. You can't just do what you like, tart around all your life. Choosing new boyfriends at every wiff and woo."

At every wiff and woo? What is she talking about? And "tarting around." That's nice talk, isn't it?

I said, "Jas, I am not a tart, I am a teenager. Just because you have thrust aside your red bottom with a firm hand and are subscribing to *Vole Weekly* doesn't make you right, you know."

She said, "Yes it does."

"No, it doesn't."

"It does."

"Jas, it doesn't make it a debate when one

person just keeps saying 'yes it does.'"

That shut her up for a nanosecond, and then she said, "Yes it does."

She is so annnnoyyyyiiing.

in my room
teatime
Robbie will be here in a minute. Blimey. I hope it doesn't rain, it's looking a bit overcast. Oh God, that has just reminded me when I first went round to Robbie's house. The very first time, I can't believe it's only a few months ago. I have become a woman since then. I have lived, loved and suffered.

one minute later
Well I've suffered and my nungas have grown quite a lot.

two minutes later
When I first met him I didn't even wear a bra. How weird is that? And stupid as it turns out, because it rained on my T-shirt and I got soaking wet when I was going round to his house. And when I looked down at my T-shirt there were two bobbles sticking

out. And it was my nip nips and I couldn't get them back in again. I had to keep my arms crossed over my nips for ages. Then he played me one of his songs and I sat there not knowing what to do, so I let an attractive (I like to think) half-smile play on my face. Unfortunately it was a long song and by the end of it my cheeks were aching quite a lot, and I was trying to keep my nose sucked in as well. I had to go to bed when I got home with face strain.

And then after all that effort the Sex God dumped me because I was too young for him and said that he knew someone that I might like called Dave the Laugh. And that is when Dave the Laugh entered stage right and I tried to use him as my decoy duck to make Robbie interested in me.

I still feel slightly bad about that bit, the decoy duck bit, especially as Dave spotted it. Actually it's quite amazing that we are mates.

two minutes later
Because that is what we are. Tip-top mates. Which is good. And how it should be.

We would have been no good as a boyfriend and girlfriend because . . . erm . . .

Well, he's not a Sex God or a Luuurve God.

He's just a sort of Dave God. And that is not on the God list. You don't have Thor and Woden and Dave, do you?

two minutes later
He is funny, though.

Ten minutes and Robbie will be ringing the doorbell. I have tarted myself up to within an inch of my life. I don't think I can stand being in the house just waiting. Maybe I will go and sit on the wall and wait for him there. Does that seem a bit keen? Yes, it does. I'll just stay here and use disciplinosity and glaciosity.

sitting on the wall
Right. What am I going to say to him? What about the snogging question? What if he wants to snog me? I can't really snog him when I am nearly officially the maybe girlfriend of a Luuurve God. Can I? We should have a snogging scale for exes. For the "once just for old time's sake" type snogging.

Mind you, I've snogged Dave the Laugh a number of times since he has been my ex. So the "just for old time's sake" rule seems to be "Yes, yes and three times yes." Well, it used to be.

Nothing has happened like that for ages. Maybe he has gone off me? I don't know why he should unless he really really likes his "girlfriend." Maybe he thinks she *is* nicer than I am. Maybe she *is* nicer than I am. But that is clearly not my fault; look at my parents.

Shutup about Dave, how did he get in here???

two minutes later
Then Robbie came round the corner and into my street. He looked very cool and sort of grown-up. I remembered all the months and months I had followed him around and dreamed of him, and gone to Stiff Dylans gigs hoping to bump into him. Or for him to talk to me. And then he had kissed me, and said we should see each other. And for a few days I had been soooooo happy. And an irresistible man magnet. And then he dumped me again! To go to Kiwi-a-gogo land and play guitar with wombats. Or was it the maracas? I didn't know.

I was about to get off the wall and say something normal(ish) to Robbie, but then he completely surprised me by just bending down and kissing me on the mouth. And not just a soft friendy kiss. A proper kiss, quite hard that lasted for about thirty seconds. My brain was chatting on about, oooh I must get a watch because Jas is sure to ask me how long I think a proper kiss lasts, and how did I know it was thirty seconds, did I time it by the sun's shadows, etc. . . . Shut up, brain, shut up.

And then just for a moment or two my brain did shut up and I just felt stuff.

Then he stopped kissing me and said, "Hi."

And I went, "Hi." Almost like a normal person.

He sat down on the wall next to me. I looked at him, and he smiled back at me.

He said, "Shall we amble down to the park, like we used to?"

in the park

It was lovely in the park. The light was filtering through the trees and making leaf shapes on the ground and there were the sounds of children laughing. I mean proper children's laughing, not like the mad heggy heggy heg heg that my sister did. Just merry little friends playing together. And a few couples holding hands and wandering about or sitting on the grass. We hadn't been talking much. I didn't mind because, to be frank, there wasn't much in my head that I wanted to let people know about. For instance I found out today in history that Shackleton, so-called hero and explorer, got stuck in the ice on his ship and so he shot his cat Mr. Chippy to make more room or make the boat lighter or something, and then they got rescued anyway! And Mr. Chippy had been the ship's cat for years and years and years. Why didn't he shoot himself if he wanted to make more room? Historical people are vair vair selfish. I must tell Dave about Mr. Chippy when I see him.

I came out of my little cat tragedy to hear Robbie saying, "Do you remember this tree, I think it was here that I sang you the song I wrote for you, do you remember?"

Yes I did, actually. And if I am honest it wasn't altogether a vair fond memory because Robbie had sort of encouraged me to put my head in his lap whilst he . . .

Robbie said, "Let's sit down for a bit, I think I can remember the words more or less . . ."

Oh no. It was all happening again. Well this time I was definitely not going to put my head on his lap.

one minute later

Oh dear God I had my head on his lap and I was once again glancing up his nostrils whilst he sang me a song about a dolphin.

in bed

10:00 p.m.

Blubbing.

I thought I had plumbed the depths of tragicosity, boywise, but I was wrong. I don't even know why I am crying really, it's just so sad. Robbie was my very first one and only Sex God and he still is, but . . . oh I don't know. He sang me the song and I did the avoiding the nostrils scenario and also I had to keep an eye on any undue nunga jiggling AND try not to let my brain run wild and free. So in the end I was all sort of tensoid and not really myself. Which of course Jas would say was a good thing.

Robbie and me snogged and did a bit of No. 6, and he is very good at it. No one can deny he is good-looking in the top-twenty sort of way. His clothes are nice. (Apart, it has to be said, from the rubber shoes from the vegetarian shop) and he did say that he and Lindsay are absolutely not an item.

And he walked me home holding my hand and when we got to my gate he kissed me really hard and long. I don't think there was any sign of virtual No. 7, but you never know.

Then he was looking at me in the moonlight (so were five other eyes until I threw my shoe at the wall and Angus, Naomi and Gordy took off). I looked at him and he had a lovely face, really lovely. And he was lovely. But . . . oh I don't know. I felt my eyes suddenly fill with tears. I couldn't help it. Everything seemed so sad, and sort of not quite right. I looked down so that he wouldn't see my blubbing.

And he stroked my hair and said, "Gee, what are you thinking?"

Oh no, what was I thinking?

I just blurted out, "Well, you left me and you have been gone so long, and the wombats and so on and then I, well, I started liking Masimo and he . . ."

Robbie looked really sad, and then he sat down next to me on the wall and was quiet. I didn't know what to say.

After a minute he said, "So you really like him, then?"

I couldn't make my voice work, I just nodded.

He still didn't say anything. I looked sideways at him. He was looking straight ahead, and as I looked a little tear came out of his eye and slipped slowly down his face. Ohhhhhhhh this was unbearable.

I was going to say, *No, no, don't cry, I'll go out with you. Anything, but don't cry.* . . . But I still couldn't make my voice work.

And then he sort of cleared his throat and said, "Georgia, don't feel bad. It's always tough to hurt someone and tell them the truth. I know that. You're a really lovely girl. Lovely . . . mad . . . but lovely. I'll always like you. Don't worry."

There was another little pause. And then he stood up and said, "Anyway, I suppose you'd better be off, you've probably got a train to catch."

At least he smiled when he said that. Which was good because I could feel the old waterworks coming on big-time.

midnight

The long and the long of it is that he is going back to New Zealand. He says there is a girl that likes him there. I stopped myself from saying "Is it Wilma the Wombat," but it did make me feel a bit funny to think of him with someone else. And also him going away again.

Oh I don't know. Would I want to go out with him if he was staying?

It's all very well writing books about how to make any twit fall in love with you, but what do you do when you have got them? That should be book two, *What to Do with a Collection of Twits When You Have Accidentally Done What Some Fool in a Book Told You to Do and Now They Are All Hanging About with You.*

12:05 a.m.
Rosie and Sven seem happy together. And they are, as we know, planning to marry in eighteen years' time. But will they? They quite clearly have nothing in common, besides snogging, snogging, snacks, mad dancing and snogging. But perhaps that is a good relationship.

Who knows?

And then there is Jas'n'Tom. They have far far too much in common, but they seem happy.

one minute later
The only thing is, to be happy like Jas I would

actually have to be Jas.

No, I just cannot go there.

I have to be me.

And I have to face the fact that I have sounded my cosmic horn and therefore my red bottomosity has led me into the oven of luuurve, onto the rack of pain and out again onto the horns of a whatsit.

Oowwwww.

Well I have made my decision, now I will have to lie on it.

tent head

friday july 29th

Mum woke me at 8:30 a.m.

"Gee, can I borrow your leather skirt, you won't be taking it on the camping trip, will you?"

I was blinking in the blinding light because she had ripped my curtains open and was scrabbling through my wardrobe.

"Mum, why would you want to borrow my leather skirt and who are you lending it to? Which incidentally you can't."

Damn! I had broken my vow of silence!!!

Mum said, "I'm not lending it to anyone, the girls and I are going to another of Uncle Eddie's gigs on Saturday. It's a sort of showcase thing and there will be him as the baldy-o-gram, there's a Viking Thor-o-gram, a Postman Pat–o-gram and there is a —"

"Mum, please stop there, as you know I am very artistic and this could send me over the edge. Are you trying to tell me that you are intending to wear my leather skirt and go watch mad blokes ponce around in their undercrackers?"

She said, "Oh no . . . they take those off as well."

How disgusting!!!

half an hour later

I've let Mum borrow my skirt and she has said that she will talk to me about Pizzaa-a-gogo land when I get back from camping. Yessssss!!!

I accidentally told her about the Robbie thing. And for her she was quite nice about it. I cried again when I told her. And I said I felt like a mean and wormy girl.

She said, "Well, it is true that you are a pain in the bum-oley most of the time. But I suppose as a teenager it's really your job. I think I was the same before I grew up."

I didn't say, *Are you mad?*

Then she went on, "Actually, I am quite proud of you. It's hard to tell the truth sometimes, especially if you don't want to hurt someone. And you did. You said what you feel. And you must do what is right for you, not what other people say is right."

She gave me a big hug and to my amazement, I gave her a spontaneous kiss. Which surprised both of us.

11:00 a.m.

We have to be at Stalag 14 to meet the coach at 3:00 p.m. I wonder if I just didn't turn up they would bog off without me. I doubt it. I should think they would send out a hanging party led by Mr. Attwood and Wet Lindsay. Ooooh I cannot believe I have to go on this ludicrous camping thing.

It's pointless taking any beauty products because unless I suddenly go mad and start fancying Herr Kamyer, there will be no other males around, apart from Miss Wilson. I am just going to bung some jumpers and jeans in a bag with some essential snacks and hope that I can sleep through the next two days. Maybe I could get one of the ace gang to hit me over the head with something and knock me out and I could wake up smiling on Sunday.

I wonder if Wet Lindsay knows that Robbie is going back to Kiwi-a-gogo land. She will go ballisticisimus. So every cloud has a silver lining.

2:00 p.m.

Lugging my bag up the hill to Stalag 14. Jas has scampered ahead because Tom is helping her carry her things to school. She's only phoned me four times to tell me how excited she is. I said to her in a moment of lighthearted repartee, "Jas, have you got a special toothbrush mug?"

And she said, "Of course, who hasn't?"

stalag 14
Things have gone horribly wrong already. Herr Kamyer is wearing shorts. That cannot be right. Or even allowed. I tried not to look at his legs. They are incredibly pale and have sort of ginger hair on them. Erlack.

We piled onto the coach and the ace gang secured the back seats. Rosie said, "We could moon the drivers behind us."

She is a sophisticate and no mistake. Tom waved us off and Jas cried and blew him kisses. What has she got to cry about? She hasn't been in the mangle of love like me.

Miss Wilson is delirious with excitement, her bob is practically dropping off. As we drove off, she stood up and said to us all, "Now then, girls, just to get us in the mood, shall we sing a few songs? What about ten green bottles?"

Is she mad?

But then we discovered that we had a bus-driving Mr. Attwood at the wheel, because he said to her, "There is no singing on the bus, madam, without the full permission of the vehicle transportation facilitator."

Miss Wilson said, "Erm, well, when, er, who is the vehicle, erm, facilitator?"

Mr. Grumpy Arse said, "Me."

And Miss Wilson said, "Well can we, erm, would it be alright for us to sing a few songs to . . ."

He just said, "No," and accelerated so hard that Miss Wilson fell over and onto Herr Kamyer's knee.

We all went "Whey hey!!!"

an hour later

I told the ace gang about the Robbie evening.

They were all going "Oh that is so sad" and so on. And it was.

Even Jas put her arm round me. I gave her a little brave smile.

It is quite tough being a boy magnet, actually. More tiring than you would think.

Then Jas said, "Well I hope you have done the right thing. If Masimo decides you are too silly to go out with, you will be on the shelf of life again."

I didn't even bother replying to her, she is so annoying. I just pulled her stupid outdoors camping hat down over her eyes.

half an hour later

In the middle of nowhere in the middle of a field. What is the point of that? Jas is practically skipping around with excitement. She went off to "explore" in the woods. Or Twig heaven, as some people might call it.

I went to look at the bathroom facilities.

ten minutes later

I said to the ace gang, "I will not be going for a poo for the next two days and that is a fact."

The "bathroom facilities" are some chemical toilets and a sort of overhead tap that is supposed to be a "shower" in some crap hut thing. I wouldn't be surprised if a pig pops its head up the lavatory pan when you sit down. Not that I will be sitting down.

I said to Miss Wilson, "This is inhumane treatment of youth. I want to make a complaint to the European Court of Human Rights, get them on the blower."

Miss Wilson said, "Well, of course, yes things are rather basic. But that is half the fun of it. I remember when I was a girl, we went camping and there were no toilet facilities at all. We had to take our little spades and dig a hole in the woods for our bowel movements."

Oh oh, Miss Wilson had mentioned her poo in front of me!!! I feel abused and dirty.

an hour later
Rosie and Jools and I are still trying to put the sodding tent up. I said to Herr Kamyer (who is sitting on a deck chair outside his tent, which even has a sort of awning over the opening), "Herr Kamyer, as you are so gut at putting stuff up, why don't you put ours up?"

And he said, "I zink it vill be more satisfactory for you if you achieve this thing yourself. It is gut for the personality."

Well he is very very wrong if he thinks that the fact that you can put a tent up is good for your personality. For instance, the people who have put their tents up are him, Miss Wilson and Jas. That speaks volumes in my book.

* * *

Jas is incredibly irritating, even for her. And that is really saying something. She is scampering around like a fool, and doing her teacher botty kissing thing. She said to Herr Kamyer, "Herr Kamyer, shall I go foraging for firewood for the fire?"

And he said, "Vat a gut idea, Jas. Do you know the right kind of vood to look for?"

Jas said, "Ooh yes, Herr Kamyer, Tom, well, he's my boyfriend, we often have fires when we go out rambling. In fact we went on a special fire-making course, so actually I can make a fire without matches."

I felt like shouting, *WHO CARES??? JUST PUT OUR BLOODY TENT UP FOR US, YOU TWIGGY TWIT!!!*

half an hour later

At last we have got our tent up and are sitting in it. Is this it? Is this what people go on and on about? Sitting in a pokey thing looking at a field?

ten minutes later

God I'm bored. When's tea?

I went over to Jas's tent and knocked on the

flap. Which I thought was amusing. Jas popped her head through the gap.

"What do you want? Your tent looks a bit of a funny shape."

I said, "Don't start me on things that look a bit of a funny shape, Jas. What are you doing in your tent? What are we supposed to do? Let me see."

She said, "Well, be careful where you put your big fat feet, it's all nice and organized in here."

Blimey. They really did have personal tooth-brush mugs.

Jas said, "I've already found a great crested newt in one of the pools by the river."

I looked at her ironically, but she didn't get it.

Babbling on and on like Lord Baden-Powell.

"Miss Wilson took a microscope with us to the pools and there were some hydra around the edge and—"

I interrupted her, "Jas, I believe I may have mentioned that I am not interested in great crested newts."

"Crested."

"Whatever. Crusted, toasted, fried—I am and will always remain a newt-free area. Have you got any snacks stashed around your person? I'm really peckish."

I made her give me one of her secret Jammy Dodgers, which she had hidden inside her owl pillowcase. Honestly.

darkness falls on the camping fiasco

As it got toward dusk, Herr Kamyer and Miss Wilson started busily getting pans out and lit a fire.

Miss Wilson said, "Girls, you will notice that Herr Kamyer has made a fire break between the fire and the meadow. One must always be aware of the danger of forest fires in high summer."

Oh yes indeedy, forest fires are high on my list of worries. Has she any idea what my luuurve life is like?

half an hour later

Actually I hate to say this, but it really is quite good fun sitting round the old campfire eating *spangleferkel* and beans from tin plates. I don't know why, but I felt a rawhide moment coming on.

I said that to Rosie and Jools. "I feel a touch of the cowboy coming on."

Rosie said, "Oo-er, shall we do a bit of cattle rustling after supps to fill in the long hours until we can get back to civilization and snogging?"

I said, "Alrighty."

So we are going to skip off and find some cows to rustle after our fruit tarts. Leave it.

fifteen minutes later

Us "campers" were all sitting around the fire as some of the eager beavers, i.e. twits and fools, went to wash the plates in the river. Jas was of course one of them. Laughing and giggling and saying stuff like, "Why, isn't that a meadowlark? And I think I spotted a badger trail. It will be exciting to watch for them tonight." Absolute tosh. Why is she so happy in the outdoors? Perhaps she has a touch of the wild pig in her gene bank. When everything was stashed away in stashing land, Herr Kamyer said, "Now then, girls, ve haf now the entertainment."

I said, "Yes, I was wondering where the TV would be plugged in."

Herr Kamyer said, "*Nein*, we have something *sehr* better, besides which I haf not got any equipment."

Oh we laughed. I must be giddy with crying and fresh air because I couldn't stop hooting with laughter for ages. Whilst Herr Kamyer just looked at us in bewilderment.

"Vat is the joke about? Why when I say I haf no equipment do you laugh? Anyway, for ze entertainment, Miss Wilson has brought some cocoa tins and we vill fill them with der rice like so."

He got a tin and filled it with rice and then Miss Wilson started filling other ones. Then the worst thing in the world happened. They started shaking them like maracas and singing "Tie Me Kangaroo Down, Sport." By Rolf Harris.

Oh it was awful.

When they tried to get everyone to join in, shaking the tins and so on, I said, "Well I am just going see what the cows are doing on this fine evening."

Rosie and Jools leapt to their feet saying, "We'll come. We'll come."

ten minutes later
We couldn't find any cows. Well actually there were some, but the field was about a hundred miles away. Anyway I didn't want to see them

really, I just wanted to rustle them.

There were some dozy-looking sheep nearer, though, so we went into their field. Blimey, sheep poo a lot. Like little pellet things. Angus would love it here, things to chase and annoy, poo, sausages, tiny innocent voley things to massacre. Cat heaven.

Rosie has decided to "improvise" cattle rustling using the sheep and her wedding horns.

eight minutes later
Rosie strapped the bison horns onto a sheep with some of her tights and she is attempting to ride it like a sort of mustang. The sheep stands there in its horns and when Rosie gets nearly on it, just shuffles away a bit. She came at it from its bottom end and managed to stay on it for a second before plunging into some sheep poo. What hilarious country larks we are having.

9:00 p.m.
Surely it must be time for bed now? The sheep were no fun. In the end they just huddled together at the far end of the field. How dim can animals be? We headed back for the campfire because we had nothing else to do. The nearest village is about

an hour away and that is probably full of the elderly insane.

9:12 p.m.
After the excitement of the singing fiasco, the atmosphere really hotted up because for our further "entertainment" Herr Kamyer started doing shadow animals in his tent with a lamp. He said people couldn't get enough of it when he went camping in the Black Forest. Do we know any German comedians? "No" is the answer you are searching for. Anyway, live and let live, I say. Herr Kamyer would make the shape and then we would have to guess what it was. Jas was keen as mustard, she got the rabbit, and the eagle, etc. On and on it went. I don't know how anyone knew what animals they were supposed to be when it was clearly just Herr Kamyer's hands.

9:20 p.m.
Then he said from inside his tent, "I zink that is enough, girls, I finish now."

And he reached to get something from his haversack. You could see him all silhouetted in the tent. I shouted out, "Erm, an elephant."

He said, "Ach no I haf now finished, I am not making the animals anymore."

And he came out of his tent with his toothbrush.

Rosie said, "A llama on holiday."

Herr Kamyer started going over to the "bathroom facilities."

"*Nein, nein,* I have finished now."

As he went into the facilities I yelled, "A Koch!" But he didn't hear me.

Jas did, though. Jas, representative for the Wildlife of Great Britain club, said, "You are being silly, Georgia. I'm off to the hide now to see if I can see any badgers. Anyone want to come with me?"

Is she insane?

two minutes later
Actually, amazingly some people did go with her.

Is it time for bed yet?

Rosie, Jools and I went into our tent and got into our sleeping bags. The tent is a bit droopy and saggy. I couldn't actually see Rosie in her sleeping bag because of the droopy bit in the middle. And she is next to me. Ah well.

I will never be able to sleep for all the hooting

and scurrying going on. And that's just Jas. . . .
Zzzzzzzzzzzzzzzzzzzzzzzzzzzz.

midnight

The tent collapsed. I woke up struggling with what felt like a big duvet and couldn't see a thing. I could hear muffled voices and Rosie saying, "I've gone blind, I've gone blind!!!"

Eventually we managed to get free of the tent and stood shivering in our pajamas. All the other tents were in darkness and I could hear snoring from Miss Wilson's tent. I wonder what she sleeps in? Can you get corduroy pajamas? Well if anyone can, she can.

I said, "I'm not going through all that putting-the-tent-up-again fiasco. We will have to crawl in with our best mateys."

ten minutes later

Jas is sooooooo unreasonable. We crawled into her tent and I tried to squeeze into her sleeping bag with her, but she wouldn't let me. Then Rosie trod on the special toothbrush mug and all hell broke loose.

12:30 a.m.

In the end, Mrs. Grumpy Knickers and her gang put our tent back up again just to get rid of us. It wasn't as droopy this time. Jas said, "You had the main tent pole in the wrong place."

So? What is that supposed to mean?

1:00 a.m.

I am dying to go to the loo. I made Rosie come with me. Pooooooooo. How horrible is it sitting on a sort of box full of stinky stuff in a tent? Vair vair horrible. It makes Gordy's kitty litter box seem like luxury.

saturday july 30th

morning

What a racket: birds chirping, cows mooing, sheep bleating. People jogging. Oh yes. That is a sight for sore eyes first thing in the morning, Miss Wilson and Herr Kamyer in their running shorts. Good Lord.

I looked in my mirror. Yep, tent head.

I don't care, though, as this is deffo a Sex God–free zone.

afternoon

An action-packed day full of getting up, eating more sausages, having to play a game of rounders.

Actually I must say I did quite enjoy that—I socked the ball into a marshy bit and Jas had to go and get it.

She said to me, "You did that on purpose."

And I said, "Don't be so silly, Jas."

And then next time I was in, I smacked the ball into exactly the same place. *Zut alors!!!*

Herr Kamyer showed us how to make a hammock and Miss Wilson told us how to identify poisonous fruits of the forest, which she couldn't find, and ended up having to show us pictures of in a book.

I said to Ellen and the gang, "The whole forest can be poisonous for all I care. I will never be coming into the wilderness again anyway."

Rosie and I managed to escape the forced march to the newt pond by slipping off and finding a tree that we could climb and hide in. We hoisted ourselves up and we could look down at the "merry campers" scampering around looking at stuff and drawing it. How anyone can be interested in drawing amoebas—I will never know. Why would you bother coming miles and miles into Nowheresville when you could get much the same effect at home drawing some snot?

3:00 p.m.

It was nice and dreamy up in the tree, actually; the sun was lovely and warm and we could stretch out on a branch in our shorts. I could do tanning work, so at least I wasn't completely wasting my time. Rosie was plaiting her hair into tiny little plaits.

I said to her, "It makes you look like a halfwit."

And she said, "Really? It looks that nice?"

Then she started missing Sven.

"Are my lips shrinking?"

I looked at them.

"No."

"They feel like they are. I've been snogging Sven every day for months."

I said, "Don't you do anything else?"

Rosie looked at me.

"Of course we do."

"What?"

"Pardon?"

"What do you do?"

"We make things—furry shorts, Viking drinking boots and so on. It's not an easy life being the bride-to-be of a Viking, you know," and she fished out her beard and put it on.

Just then we heard some voices and had to

shut up so that no one would see us. We could see down through the leaves. It was Miss Wilson and Herr Kamyer. Both in shorts. Good grief.

Herr Kamyer said, "It is *ver varm nicht var*?"

Miss Wilson was dithering about with a towel, and said, "Yes indeed, I think I'll have a refreshing shower." And she bounded off to the "bathroom facilities."

Herr Kamyer busied himself with his magnifying glass. I think he was trying to start a fire with it. What is the point of that?

Rosie whispered, "I do hope he sets fire to his shorts."

five minutes later

Some of the merry campers have come back from the newt pond and are having another game of rounders. Nauseating P. Green, who has been keeping a low profile this weekend, thank the Lord, is a fielder out by the bathroom facility.

I said to Rosie quietly, "I don't want to be mean or anything, but Nauseating P. Green is unusually unusual-looking."

Rosie stopped plaiting for a minute to look. "Please let her fall over. There's nothing funnier than seeing her trying to get up again."

At which point Melanie Griffiths socked the rounders ball really hard over to where N. P. Green was on fielding duties. Melanie ran for first base, and even Herr Kamyer stopped setting fire to things to look up. As I may have mentioned before, Melanie's nunga-nungas have a life of their own when she's running.

I said to Rosie, "Any minute now she will come careening past us and into the woods."

Everyone was shouting at N. P. Green. "Catch the ball, four eyes, catch it!"

I said, "She can't even see the ball. The ball would have to be the size of her arse to see it through those glasses."

At which point the funniest thing known to humanity happened.

N. P. Green was running backward, trying to catch where she thought the ball might be, and she crashed into the bathroom facility. Half of the bathroom facility (also known as a piece of old tent) collapsed around her, to reveal Miss Wilson blinking out from underneath the shower.

Rosie and I nearly fell out of the tree.

three minutes later

My ribs hurt from laughing. Seeing Miss Wilson in the nuddy-pants, apart from a spotted shower cap, is possibly the sight of the century. She just stood there blinking in the sun with her soap on a rope.

Rosie said, "Cor!"

ten minutes later

Miss Wilson managed to crawl under the rest of the bathroom facility and has just come out with her clothes on.

As she came out, Herr Kamyer walked quickly into the woods.

five minutes later

I said to Rosie, "Imagine if it had been Slim."

Rosie said, "No."

ten minutes later

Miss Wilson is fiddling about near the cooking area, and Herr Kamyer has just come out of the woods whistling. Miss Wilson is pointing across to the bathroom facility. Herr Kamyer is taking off his glasses, pointing at the bathroom facility and shrugging his shoulders. It's like watching mime.

Then I got it. "Herr Kamyer is pretending that he did not see Miss Wilson in the rudey-dudeys!"

one minute later

Back to the important things of life. I said to Rosie, "I wonder if I did the right thing about the Sex God. I wonder if I do like Masimo more than him."

She said, "You've got to get your priorities right in life."

Blimey, she was getting a bit deep for someone who was sporting a head full of tiny plaits and a full beard.

I said, "How do you mean?"

"Well, to put it another way. Who is the best snogger?"

Hmmmmmmmmmm.

two minutes later

I gave Masimo 9 out of 10 for snogging, and Robbie 8.

Rosie said, "Well, there you are, then."

Yes, when you put it like that.

Then she said, "What is the best snog you have ever had? Don't think about it, just say what comes into your head."

Blimey. I've just said something that has amazed even me.

"I think it was when Dave the Laugh nibbled my lips."

Rosie looked at me and scratched her beard.

"How did Dave the Laugh get in here?"

Good point, well made.

in our tent
9:00 p.m.

Well, nearly time to get back to civilization. I can still hear the rest of the campers around the fire. Rosie, Jools and me are all in our sleeping bags. I have got some choccy and we are trying to suck it and see who can make it last the longest. That is how exciting life is. As we were lying there sucking we heard a sort of scrabbling at the side of the tent and then a hand came looming into view at the bottom of the canvas. We were being plundered, probably by farmers.

I said, "Oy, why don't you bog off back to where you came from? I have a gun."

And a voice said, "Yes, but what color pants have you got on?"

It couldn't be?

It was though.

Dave the Laugh, Tom, Sven, Rollo and Dec and another mate called Edward I didn't know had all come down in Tom's car to visit us. They were camped just down the road by the river.

Yes, yes, yes!!!

We were talking quietly to them through the tent wall.

Dave said from the other side of the tent, "If you pretend to go to the loo, you can all come back in and say good night to the teachers like you are going to sleep for the night, and then burrow out the back of the tent and come with us. For a laugh. You know you want to!"

He is such a cheeky cat. How exciting, though!

Tom's voice said, "Get Jas to come out as well."

Dec said, "Yeah, and get two other ones."

I said, "Two other what?"

Dec said, "Girls."

Boys are really unbelievable.

I'm sure Mabs and Ellen are not going to come out and just be with some blokes who call them "two other ones." Even Ellen has got a bit of pride-nosity. Ish.

The lads told us how to get to their campsite

and said they would wait for us there. We got into our clothes and then put our dressing gowns over the top of them. Jools, Rosie and I trooped over to the now re-erected loos, passing by the fire where the rest of them were singing "Ging gang gooley gooley gooley."

Fortunately Rosie had thought to bring emergency makeup supplies and when we got in the "loos" (poo-ey) I had a quick look in the mirror. My tent hair had calmed down a bit during the day, and I did a mascara, lippy, lip gloss thing. Rosie was leaping about undoing her plaits and practicing puckering up. Jools said, "So what is the plan?"

I said, "Here's the plan, we go back to the tent yawning. And pretend we are shattered from having so much camping fun that we are having an early night. Then we burrow under the bottom of the tent and sneak off down to the boys' camp for fun and frolics and snacks."

Rosie said, "And snogging."

Jools said, "How shall we get the rest of them away from the ging gang goolie fiasco?"

I said, "We must use sophisticosity and *je ne sais quoi*."

When we got back to the campfire, the "party"

was still on. Herr Kamyer was showing the campers how to do some ludicrous knots. What is the point of that? When was the last time anyone used a knot? I think it might have been Admiral Nelson. As we passed by yawning like the Yawners of Yawnington, I said in a casualosity-at-all-times way, "Oh Jas, Ellen and Mabs, I forgot I . . . er . . . have something to show you in our tent."

Jas looked at me and didn't even bother to reply.

Ellen said, "Oh right, shall we, erm . . . is it . . . can I . . . are we all . . ."

And so on.

I gave Jas my most meaningful look, but she didn't know what I meant.

I said, "We found it this afternoon. I think it might be quite good for your newt collection, Jas."

She said, "Is it a crusted one, or a toasted one?"

And she didn't say it in a nice way.

I was about to do stormies off, but then I thought I might have to listen to her ramble and moan on for the rest of my life if she found out that Tom had been here and I hadn't told her.

So I said, "Oh I think you will find it quite

HUNKY, if you know what I mean, Jas."

That got her attention alright. She leapt to her feet like a surprised loon.

I said, looking at her with my eyes really wide, "Why don't you all pop round to our tent for a good night, er, look at it?"

We all trooped off to our tent. Miss Wilson said, "Don't be up all night chattering, girls, it's been quite a day and you're all very excited, I expect. I know I am."

Everyone looked at each other and tried not to laugh.

Miss Wilson was still burbling on, "Did you have an exciting day, Herr Kamyer?"

And Herr Kamyer looked at her and said, "Yeah, it was ver exciting."

Oh my giddy god, please don't tell me Herr Kamyer has the Horn for Miss Wilson.

Life is too weird for me and I've only been on the planet for a bit.

back in our tent

It was very crowded in the tent. I took off my dressing gown and Jas, Ellen and Mabs had a go on the emergency makeup supplies. When they were sufficiently tarted up, we started our burrowing tactics. It was dark by now and we had to switch off our lights so that you couldn't see us burrowing. Actually when I say burrowing what I mean is pulling up the canvas so that we could scamper under it out into freedom!!!

We crept along the back of the campsite, keeping to the treeline.

in the boys' tent

They have got a big green one (oo-er). It was quite groovy in it, even though it was a tent. When we put our heads through the flap, the boys cheered and offered us some pizza they had got from the village. Yum yum. Sven immediately almost ate Rosie and then sat on her knee. Dec snuggled up to Ellen who went bright red (even in the dark) and Edward said hello to Mabs. She was pleased because her blind date was a) not blind and b) very fit looking. Tom and Jas went off to the river because Jas said, "Tom, come and see the badger hide, it's amazing."

I laughed ironically, but she just looked at me and went off with Hunky.

Dave patted the ground next to him.

"Come and sit down, kittykat, you must be exhausted from all the fun you have been having."

half an hour later

What a hoot and a half. Dave does make me laugh. I'd forgotten how groovy he can be. Ellen and Dec and Mabs and Edward seemed to be grooving along together. Quite nice to see Ellen not watching Dave like a Seeing Eye dog.

Dave played some music and we had a mini disco inferno in the tent.

It was hysterically funny, actually. We had to dance really close to each other and sort of do it half bending over. If you see what I mean.

twenty minutes later

Naturally Sven made the tent collapse with a reckless diving tackle on Dave at a fast bit. I could hardly stand for laughing.

The lads put the tent up again and I was resting with Dave by some bushes.

Dave said to me, "Do you fancy a quick swim in the nuddy-pants?"

I said, "You're mad."

He looked at me. "You're mad."

"No, you're mad."

Then he just pushed me over into a bush.

I said as I got up, "You can't do that, that is assault and battery."

He said, "No, wrong, kittykat, this is assault and battery."

And he pushed me into the bush again!!!

Then he said, "I'll count to ten and then I am coming to get you."

"Dave, I'm not going anywhere."

He said, "I would if I were you, anyway if you don't go anywhere how can I come and get you?"

I don't know why but it seemed to make sense, so I started jogging off. What was I doing? As usual, I would be the last to know. I bet I could outrun Dave anyway.

five minutes later

Wrong.

He caught up with me at the river. I stuck my feet in it I was so hot. Dave came and sat down next to me and put his feet in as well. It was a beautiful dark night, and the air was soft and warm. I felt really happy and relaxed.

I know I shouldn't have, but you know when you

shouldn't say anything but you still say it? Well I had that. I said, "How, erm, how is your girlfriend situation-type fandango going?"

He looked at me and half-smiled. "How is your maybe two boyfriends fandango going, missy?"

I didn't know what to say. Then I blurted out, "Well, Robbie said he liked me, but then I told him I liked Masimo, but Masimo wants me to go to Pizza-a-gogo land, and really it should be groovy and so on, but I don't really know."

Dave said, "You don't know what, kittykat?"

Oh I wish I could just put my head on his shoulder. I always want to tell him everything. But instead I said, "What's your advice, Hornmeister?"

And he started doing pretend beard stroking and said, "Well, luuurve is a many trousered thing. . . ."

What in the name of arse does that mean? I repeated, "Luuurve is a many trousered thing? That is your idea of advice?"

Dave said, "Well, put it another way, maybe you like more than one pair of trousers. Maybe you like Masimo and maybe someone else . . ."

What exactly were we talking about now?

He went on, "Yes, for instance, I like Emma, but I like someone else, possibly better."

I couldn't help myself, even though I knew this was dangerous red-bottom territory. I said, "Who else might you like?"

After a pause he said, "The queen," and stood up.

I was looking up at him. I said, "You like the queen? The other person you like maybe more is the queen? The queen who's just celebrated her eightieth birthday? The queen? The one who's had her hips replaced?"

He said, "That was her mother, actually. Please don't be rude about my girlfriend."

I stood up, but I couldn't quite see in the dark and I put my foot down some bloody badger hole or a twig trap that Miss Wilson had made or something and I fell backward. Into the edge of the river.

Dave was laughing, but he came to help me up out of the riverbank. "Oh you are good value, Georgia. You are very nearly an honorary bloke. And that is why I love you."

Did he—did he just say what I thought he'd said? He reached down and put his arms round my waist to lift me up. I hope he didn't feel my wet knickers and think I'd had an elderly loon moment.

He said, "Have you wet yourself, Gee? Your knickers are soaking."

I said, "No, but I think they're full of tadpoles, and actually my bum-oley really hurts."

As he pulled me up the bank, I said, "I think I may have broken my bottom."

He looked at my face and he was really smiling. Then he said, "Are we never to be free, kittykat?"

And I looked at him and he said, "Oh bugger it, it has to be done."

And he snogged me.

Oh no. I've just unexpectedly paid a visit to the cakeshop of love. I haven't put back my Italian cakey, but I've accidentally picked up a Dave the Tart.

The Ace Gang

Proper and Official Members

Georgia—*Moi*. The pièce de résistance. Bee's knees, etc.

Jas—Supposed best pally. Prone to rambling on. Wears enormous pantaloonies.

Rosie—A Viking bride to be. Known for her beards and eccentric dancing.

Jools—Good in an emergency, e.g., usually has secret lippy supply.

Ellen—Ditherqueen of the universe and beyond.

Mabs—Generally all-round good egg. Keen on snogging and snacking.

Honorary Bloke Members

Dave the Laugh—Famously said he would like to be a girl so he could look at his nunga-nungas all day. Also known as the Hornmeister.

Tom—Brother of the Sex God and Jas's

"boyfriend." Actually, as boys go, not entirely mad.

Sven—from Reindeer land (possibly). Spectacularly mad, e.g., wears flares that have flashing lights down the seams.

Trainee Members

Honor and Soph—Coming on nicely. Already involved in the snot disco triumph and the hilarious putting a skeleton dressed as Mr. Atwood in his hut.

Groove on, groovsters!

In case you haven't noticed, me and the ace gang have created some of the grooviest dance moves ever invented. I always find that a quick burst of disco inferno dancing is a fab way of getting rid of tensionosity and frustrated snoggosity. So because I love you all so much, I have written down our fave steps so you can get grooving too.

The Viking bison disco inferno

We're still practicing this for Rosie's forthcoming (i.e., in 18 years' time) Viking wedding. It is danced to the tune of *Jingle Bells* because even Rosie, world authority on Sven land, doesn't know any Viking songs. Apart from *Rudolph the Red-nosed Reindeer*. Which isn't one.

For this dance you need some bison horns. If you can't find any bison shops nearby, make your own horns from an old hairband and a couple of twigs or something. Oh, I don't know, stop hassling me. I'm tired.

Instructions:
Stamp, stamp to the left,
Left leg kick, kick,
Arm up,
Stab, stab to the left (that's the pillaging bit),
Stamp, stamp to the right,
Right leg kick, kick,
Arm up,
Stab, stab to the right,
Quick twirl round with both hands raised to
Thor (whatever)
Raise your (pretend) drinking horn to the left,
Drinking horn to the right,
Horn to the sky,
All over body shake
Huddly duddly,
And fall to knees with a triumphant shout of
"HORRRRNNNNN!!!!"

P.S.
In a rare moment of comic genius, Jas, who is
clearly in touch with her inner bison, added this bit
too—it's a sort of sniffing the air type move. Like a

Viking bison might do. If it was trying to find its prey. And if there was such a thing as a Viking bison.

Stab, stab to the left,
And then sniff sniff.

Hahahahahaha!

The snot disco inferno

For this dance you will need a big blob of bubble gum hanging off your nose like a huge bogey. It needs to dangle about so you can swing it round and round in time to the music. Dance this to the tune of *EastEnders*, or your favorite TV show theme tune. It goes:

Swing your snot to the left,
Swing to the right.
Full turn,
Shoulder shrug,
Nod to the front,
Dangle dangle,
Hands on shoulders,
Kick, kick to the right,

Dangle dangle,
Kick, kick to the left,
Dangle dangle,
Full snot around,
And shimmy to the ground.

Excellent in every way!

The New and Improved Snogging Scale

$^1/_2$. sticky eyes (Be careful using this. I've still got some complete twit following me around like a seeing-eye dog.)

1. holding hands
2. arm around
3. goodnight kiss
4. kiss lasting over three minutes without a breath (What you need for this is a sad mate who's got a watch but no boyfriend.)

$4\,^1/_2$. hand snogging (I really don't want to go into this. Ask Jas.)

5. open mouth kissing
6. tongues

$6\,^1/_2$. ear snogging

$6\,^3/_4$. neck nuzzling

7. upper body fondling—outdoors
8. upper body fondling—indoors (in bed)

Virtual number 8. When your upper body is not actually being fondled in reality, but you know that it is in your snoggee's head.

9. below waist activity (or bwa) (Apparently this can include flashing your pants. Don't blame me. Ask Jools.)

10. the full monty (Jas and I were in the room when Dad was watching the news and the newscaster said, "Tonight the Prime Minister has reached Number 10." And Jas and I had a laughing spaz to end all laughing spazzes.)

Glossary

airing cupboard • It's a cupboard full of air, you fools. If you haven't got enough air, you go into the airing cupboard in your house. Not really! It's a cupboard by the hot water boiler and you put towels and sheets in and they get all warm and snuggly buggly (don't start saying you don't know what snuggly buggly means).

arvie • Afternoon. From the Latin "arvo." Possibly. As in the famous Latin invitation: "Lettus meetus this arvo."

Black Death • Ah well . . . this is historiosity at its best. In Merrie England, everyone was having a fab time, dancing about with bells on (also known as Maurice dancing), then some ships arrived in London, full of new stuff—tobacco, sugar, chocolate, etc., yum yum. However, as in all tales in history, it ended badly, because also lurking about on the ships were rats from Europe—not human ones. And they had fleas on them that carried the plague. The fleas bit the people of Merrie England, and they got covered in pustulating boils and died. A LOT. As I have said many many times, history is crap.

Blimey O'Reilly • (as in "Blimey O'Reilly's trousers")

This is an Irish expression of disbelief and shock. Maybe Blimey O'Reilly was a famous Irish bloke who had extravagantly big trousers. We may never know the truth. The fact is, whoever he is, what you need to know is that a) it's Irish and b) it is Irish. I rest my case.

blodge • Biology. Like geoggers—geography—or Froggie—French.

bloke • You must know what a bloke is . . . it is a person of the masculine gender. Hence the expression "my bloke"—as in "I am dumping my bloke because he is too thick."

boboland • As I have explained many, many times English is a lovely and exciting language full of sophisticosity. To go to sleep is "to go to bobos," so if you go to bed you are going to boboland. It is an Elizabethan expression (oh, OK then, Libby made it up and she can be unreasonably violent if you don't join in with her).

bugger • A swear word. It doesn't really mean anything but neither do a lot of swear words. Or parents.

bum-oley • Quite literally bottom hole. I'm sorry but you did ask. Say it proudly (with a cheery smile and a Spanish accent).

bunged • Shoved. Put firmly in place. For example, "Jas was going on and on about voles, so I bunged a Jammy Dodger in her gob."

chav • A chav is a common, rude, rough person. They

wear naff clothes. A chav joke would be, "What are the first words a chav baby says to its single parent?" Answer: "What are YOU looking at??" Or: "If there are two chavs in a car and no loud music playing, what kind of a car is it?" Answer: "A police car."

chuddie • Chewing gum. This is an "i" word thing. We have a lot of them in English due to our very busy lives, explaining stuff to other people not so fortunate as ourselves.

Cliff Richard's Y-Fronts • Y-fronts are boys' knickers, but they are not worn by any boy you would want to know. Cliff Richard is a living legend (who is now a Lord—or is it a Lady?).

clown car • Officially called a Reliant Robin three-wheeler, but clearly a car built for clowns, built by some absolute loser called Robin. The Reliant bit comes from being able to rely on Robin being a prat. I wouldn't be surprised if Robin also invented nostril hair cutters.

conk • Nose. This is very interesting historically. A very long time ago (1066)—even before my grandad was born—a bloke called William the Conqueror (French) came to England and shot our King Harold in the eye. Typical. And people wonder why we don't like the French much. Anyway, William had a big nose and so to get our own back we call him William the Big Conkerer. If you see what I mean. I hope you do because I am exhausting myself with my hilariosity and historiosity.

div • Short for "dithering prat," i.e., Jas.

DIY • Quite literally "Do It Yourself!" Rude when you think it about it. Instead of getting someone competent to do things around the house (you know, like a trained electrician or a builder or a plumber), some vatis choose to do DIY. Always with disastrous results. (For example, my bedroom ceiling has footprints in it because my vati decided he would go up on the roof and replace a few tiles. Hopeless.)

double cool with knobs • "Double" and "with knobs" are instead of saying very or very, very, very, very. You'd feel silly saying, "He was very, very, very, very, very cool." Also everyone would have fallen asleep before you had finished your sentence. So "double cool with knobs" is altogether snappier.

duffing up • Duffing up is the female equivalent of beating up. It is not so violent and usually involves a lot of pushing with the occasional pinch.

dustbins • Things to put your rubbish in. Or probably as you say in America land, refuse. Or is it garbage? Or junk? In England it is dustbin because we have a lot of dust (possibly).

Emily Plankton • Hang on, now that you mention it, I may be getting muddled up between the famous suffragette Emily Whatsit and stuff that fish eat. Was it Emily Pancake then? No, wait a minute, Pankhurst—Emily Pankhurst. What is this anyway, some kind of general knowledge quiz?

fag • Cigarette.

fandango • A fandango is a complicated Spanish dance. So a fandango is a complicated thing. Yes, I know there is no dancing involved. Or Spanish.

footie • Soccer.

form • A form is what we call class at English secondary schools. It is probably a Latin expression. Probably from the Latin "formus ignoramus."

fringe • Goofy short bit of hair that comes down to your eyebrows. Someone told me that American-type people call them "bangs" but this is so ridiculously strange that it's not worth thinking about. Some people can look very stylish with a fringe (i.e., me) while others look goofy (Jas). The Beatles started it apparently. One of them had a German girlfriend, and she cut their hair with a pudding bowl and the rest is history.

Froggie and geoggers • Froggie is short for French, geoggers is short for geography. Ditto blodge (biology) and lunck (lunch).

full-frontal snogging • Kissing with all the trimmings, lip to lip, open mouth, tongues . . . everything. (Apart from dribble, which is never acceptable.)

f.t. • I refer you to the famous "losing it" scale.
1. minor tizz
2. complete tizz and to-do

3. strop
4. a visit to Stop Central
5. F.T. (Funny turn)
6. spazattack
7. complete ditherspaz
8. nervy b. (nervous breakdown)
9. complete nervy b.
10. ballisiticisimus

gadzooks • An expression of surprise. Like for instance, "Cor, love a duck!" Which doesn't mean you love ducks or want to marry one. For the swotty knickers amongst you, "gad" probably meant "God" in olde English, and "zooks" of course means . . . Oh, look, just leave me alone, OK? I'm so vair tired.

games • Sports.

get off with • A romantic term. It means to use your womanly charms to entice a boy into a web of love. Oh OK then—snogging.

gob • Gob is an attractive term for someone's mouth. For example, if you saw Mark (from up the road who has the biggest mouth known to womankind) you could yell politely, "Good Lord, Mark, don't open your gob, otherwise people may think you are a basking whale in trousers and throw a mackerel at you" or something else full hilariosity.

goosegog • Gooseberry. I know you are looking all quizzical now. OK. If there are two people and they want to snog and you keep hanging about saying "Do you fancy some chewing gum?" or "Have you seen my interesting new socks?" you are a gooseberry. Or for short a goosegog, i.e., someone who nobody wants around.

gorgey • Gorgeous. Like fabby (fabulous) and marvy (marvelous).

havvies • Haversacks. Life is too shor to fini wor.

horn • When you "have the horn" it's the same as "having the big red bottom."

Jammy Dodger • Biscuit with jam in it. Very nutritious(ish).

jimjams • Pajamas. Also pygmies or jammies.

jumper • Pullover. Hey, do you think it is called a jumper because it is made from wool, and sheep jump about? No, neither do I.

Kiwi-a-gogo land • New Zealand. "A-gogo land" can be used to liven up the otherwise really boring names of other countries. America, for instance, is Hamburger-a-gogo land, Mexico is Mariachi-a-gogo land and France is Frogs'-legs-a-gogo land. This is from that very famous joke told every Christmas by the elderly mad (Grandad). Oh very well, I'll tell you it.

A man goes into a French restaurant and says to the French waiter, "Have you got frogs' legs?"

The waiters says, "Oui, monsieur."

And the man says, "Well, hop off and get me a sandwich then."

This should give you some idea of what our Christmases are like.

knickers • Panties, briefs, things you wear to conceal girlie parts. Boys don't wear knickers; they wear underpants or boxer shorts. Some of them wear underpants that have a Union Jack or a funny joke on them. So Jas says, but she is, as we are all too aware, mad.

lippy • Oh come on, you know what it is! Lipstick!! Honestly, what are you lot like!

loo • Lavatory. In America they say "rest room," which is funny, as I never feel like having a rest when I go to the lavatory.

Lord Baden-Powell • You don't know who Lord Baden-Powell is? Blimey you are, it has to be said, v. v. dense. Lord B-P invented Scouts and camping, and knots and going into the country for no reason. Ergo, Lord B-P was clearly mad as a hen.

P.S. Not content with the camping fiasco, he also invented enormous shorts, which he wore proudly.

lurgy • Is when you feel icky-poo. Please tell me that you know what icky-poo means. Oh good Lord. It means "poorly." Lurgy is like a bug. An illness bug, Ergo, tummy lurgy = stomach bug.

midget gem • Little sweets made out of hard jelly stuff in different flavors. Jas loves them A LOT. She secretes them about her person, I suspect, often in her panties, so I never like to accept one from her on hygiene and lesbian grounds.

milky pops • A soothing hot milk drink, when you are a little person. (No, not an elf, I mean a child.) Anyway, what was I saying? Oh yes, when you are a child, people give words endings to make them more cozy. Chocolate is therefore choccy woccy doo dah. Blanket is blankin'. Tooth is tushy peg. Easy is easy peasey lemon squeasey. If grown-ups ever talk like this, do not hesitate to kill them.

naff • Unbearably and embarrassingly out of fashion and nerdy. Naff things are: Parents dancing to "modern" music, blue eyeshadow, blokes who wear socks with sandals, pigtails. You know what I mean.

nervy spaz • Nervous spasm. Nearly the same as a nervy b. (nervous breakdown) or an f.t. (funny turn), only more spectacular on the physical side.

nippy noodles • Instead of saying "Good heavens, it's quite cold this morning," you say "Cor—nippy noodles!!" English is an exciting and growing language. It is. Believe me. Just leave it at that. Accept it.

nuddy-pants • Quite literally nude-colored pants, and you know what nude-colored pants are? They are no pants. So if you are in your nuddy-pants you are in your no pants, i.e., you are naked.

nunga-nungas • Basoomas. Girls' breasty business.

Ellen's brother calls them nunga-nungas because he says that if you get hold a girl's breast and pull it out and then let it go—it goes nunga-nunga-nunga. As I have said many, many times with great wisdomosity, there is something really wrong with boys.

Pantalitzer • A terrifying Czech-made doll that sadistic parents (my vati) buy for their children, presumably to teach them early on about the horror of life. Essentially the Pantalitzer doll has a weird plastic face with a horrible fixed smile. The rest of Pantalitzer is a sort of cloth bag with hard plastic hands on each side like steel forks.

I don't know if I have mentioned this before, but I am not reassured that Eastern Europeans really know how to have a laugh.

Pizza-a-gogo land • Masimoland. Land of wine, sun, olives and vair vair groovy Luuurve Gods. Italy. (The only bad point about Pizza-a-gogo land is their football players are so vain that if it rains, they all run off the pitch so that their hair doesn't get ruined. See also Chelsea players.)

plight my troth • Give your word luuurve-wise. Another way of saying you are my one and only one. So if you are "untrothed" you can display red bottomosity ad hoc and willy nilly.

prat • A prat is a gormless oik. You make a prat of yourself by mistakenly putting both legs down one knicker leg or by playing air guitar at pop concerts.

red bottomosity • Having the big red bottom. This is vair vair interesting *via-à-vis* nature. When a lady baboon is "in the mood" for luuurve, she displays her big red bottom to the male baboon. (Apparently he wouldn't have a clue otherwise, but that is boys for you!!) Anyway, if you hear the call of the Horn you are said to be displaying red bottomosity.

Rolf Harris • An Australian "entertainer" (not). Rolf has a huge beard and glasses. He plays a didgeridoo, which says everything in my book. He sadly has had a number of hit records, which means he is never off TV and will not go back to Australia. (His "records" are called "Tie Me Kangaroo Down, Sport," etc. . . .)

snogging • Kissing.

The Sound of Music • Oh are we never to be free? *The Sound of Music* was a film about some bint, Julie Andrews, skipping around in the Alps and singing about goats. Many many famous and annoying songs come from this film, including, "The Hills Are Alive with the Sounds of PANTS," "You Are Sixteen Going on PANTS," and, of course, the one about the national flower of Austria, "IdlePANTS."

spangleferkel • A kind of German sausage. I know. You couldn't make it up, could you? The German language is full of this kind thing, like lederhosen and so on. And Goosegot.

spot • Officially a blocked pore that gets all red and

inflamed and sometimes has a white top on it. In reality something you get every time you need to look your best. You never get spots in concealed places—they are always on your nose or chin or on a sticky-out bit. Americans call them "zits" and I hope against hope this has nothing to do with the noise they make when you pop them.

swot • A person who has no life and as a substitute has to read books and learn things for school. Also anyone who does their homework on time.

tart • A girl who is a bit on the common side. This is a tricky one, actually, because if I wear a very short skirt I am cool and sexy, However, if Jackie Bummer wears a short skirt it is a) a crime against humanity and b) tarty.

tatty bye • Now this is interesting, so gather round and get your ears on, as Yogi Bear used to say. (Don't start asking me who Yogi Bear is, otherwise we'll be here all day and night.) "Tatty" is another word for "potato" in olde English, so Mrs. Billy Shakespeare would say, "Shall we have tatties and pheasant for tea, Billy?" So when you are saying good-bye, English people say tatty bye, and it quite literally means "good-bye potato."

titches • A titch is a small person. Titches is the plural of titch.

tosser • A special kind of prat. The other way of putting this is "wanker" or "monkey spanker."

vino tinto • Now this is your actual Pizza-a-gogo talk. It quite literally means "tinted wine." In this case the wine is tinted red.

waz • Another expression for piddly diddly department. Possibly named after the sound the piddly diddly makes as it comes out of the trouser area. I don't know, to be frank. Only boys say it. And who knows why boys say anything? The whole thing is a mystery.

wazzarium • A place where you go to have a waz. P.S. You will not be finding me in there.

wet • A drippy, useless, nerdy idiot. Linday.

whelk boy • A whelk is a horrible shellfish thing that only the truly mad eat. Slimy and mucuslike. Whelk boy is a boy who kisses like a whelk, i.e., a slimy mucus kisser. Erlack a pongoes.